My Sisters's Keeper

My Sisters's Keeper

Beverly Butler

DODD, MEAD & COMPANY
NEW YORK

ACKNOWLEDGMENTS

My very warmest thanks to Mary Olsen, whose suggestion kindled the spark for this novel; to Laurene De Witt and Lil Palm, whose hospitality and interest opened invaluable doors into the life and tragedy of Peshtigo of 1871; to Margaret O'Connell, who gave without stint of her years of knowledge and the impressive resources of the Marinette County Historical Museum; to Robert W. Wells, whose book *Fire at Peshtigo* provided the springboard for this story and an ever-fascinating treasury of detail; and to T. V. Olsen, who drove, read, researched, counseled, encouraged, and forebore to a degree far and beyond the bounds of marital duty.

Printed in the United States of America

1 2 3 4 5 6 7 8 9 10

Library of Congress Cataloging in Publication Data

Butler, Beverly.
My sister's keeper.

SUMMARY: In the north woods of Wisconsin following a forest fire that destroys their town in 1871, 17-year-old Mary James forms a new respect for her older sister.
[1. Brothers and sisters—Fiction. 2. Forest fires—Fiction. 3. Survival—Fiction] I. Title.
PZ7.B974My [Fic] 79-6637
ISBN 0-396-07803-6

For the famous Muriel Butler, my mother,
and the far-famed Mary Olsen, my mother-in-law,
with love

The last thing on earth Mary James wanted was to be sent north to help out her older sister Clara who was expecting her fourth child. She arrived in the lumber town of Peshtigo, Wisconsin, in this drought year of 1871 to find shrieking sawmills, the air thick with smoke from fires in the surrounding forest, and Clara every bit as unreasonable and demanding as she remembered her. Only Ellery, Clara's husband — handsome, light-hearted, dashing — made life bearable.

The moment comes when Mary and Clara confront one another over Ellery's affections, but even that does not matter when the forest explodes into a wall of flame, and flight to safety is the only concern. In the aftermath of the fire that consumes the town and over a thousand lives, Mary's life is altered forever. Survival is far more complicated than merely staying alive through one night of terror. Tomorrow would be shaped by choices only she could make.

And the Lord said unto Cain,
Where is Abel thy brother?
And he said, I know not:
Am I my brother's keeper?

Genesis 4:9

Moreover, if thy brother shall trespass
against thee, go and tell him
his fault between thee and him alone:
if he shall hear thee,
thou hast gained thy brother.

Matthew 18:15

MARY JAMES TOOK care to sweep her trailing skirt free of the end of the pew before she followed Clara, her sister, and Clara's three children into the aisle. The dress was new. She had put the finishing stitches in it just in time to pack it into her trunk for her journey to this lumber town of Peshtigo where Clara lived, and she had no intention of allowing it to be snagged on a nail or soiled by the boot of some heavy-footed mill worker.

She glanced up and caught the eye of a round-faced young man, who had been obviously staring at her. Mary widened her own green eyes, then quickly lowered them. But not so quickly that she missed seeing the young man's ears turn pink.

She hid a little smile of satisfaction. The boys and young men up here in the north woods were going to be no different from the ones she knew back home. The combination of cream-smooth skin, a dimpled chin, hair of burnished copper, and a waist her father's two hands could circle with inches to spare had the effect of a magic wand on occasion, bestowing small attentions on her and granting her favors that other girls often had to struggle for or do without.

Even Tat, Clara's four-year-old, was walking behind his mother with his head twisted over his shoulder to be sure Mary was following. Mary gave him a smile and dropped her hands to his shoulders to help steer him straight. He began to giggle, and letting his head loll, leaned back against her, going limp all over so that she had to tighten her hold to keep him from plopping to the floor.

"Tat!" Clara said sharply without looking around. "Behave yourself."

Tat regained the use of his arms and legs at once, to Mary's quiet relief. She was not against attracting the notice of other people, but she wanted to attract it for the right reasons—admiring reasons. There was nothing to admire and certainly no dignity to remark in a young lady's wrestling a little boy gone silly. Most especially she did not care to attract that sort of notice on this, her first Sunday in the Peshtigo Congregational Church.

Still, she could not deny that in the three days since her arrival at Clara's home, Tat had become her favorite of the children. He was so much the picture of his father, who was striding ahead of them toward the door, inches taller than anyone. Tat had his father's same thick hair the color of corn silk, the same roguish sparkle in his blue eyes, the same finely molded nose and mobile mouth, the same heart-stopping grin. Perhaps one day he would possess his father's remarkable charm as well, but Mary could not quite bring herself to believe that.

There was really only one Ellery Cody; there could never be another. When he had come, still in his uniform of the Wisconsin Fourth Cavalry, to the James farm to marry Clara at the end of the war, Mary had thought him the most handsome man she had ever seen. That was in 1865, and she had been eleven. She was seventeen now, and it was six years since the wedding, but these past few days of renewed acquaintance had given her no cause to alter her earliest opinion save to admit that he had grown more handsome and more charming than she remembered. His presence was the only bright spot she foresaw in the next two or three months that she would have to endure as a glorified hired girl in her sister's house.

Unfortunately, six years of marriage had left Clara almost exactly as Mary remembered her too. Mary cast a bleak glance at the uncompromising straightness of her sister's spine. Clara was propelling two-year-old Ida ahead of her with one hand and towing five-year-old Netty after her with the other. Netty was still sniffling from having had her thumb slapped from her mouth just before the final "Amen."

"I warned you," Clara told her without attempting to modulate her voice. "If you are going to act like a baby, you'll get treated like one."

A body would suppose that Clara would be so proud and grateful to have a husband like Ellery that nothing else would matter much, especially when Clara herself was such a plain woman. She took after Pa's side of the family: big of bone and square of face. In fact, she looked a lot like Pa's mother, which was probably why he tended to favor her at unaccountable times. Not even Pa, though, could have dreamed that she would have the luck to attract a man who could have had his pick of any dozen girls he chose.

But every line of Clara's figure, far from radiating appreciation of her good fortune, was set in the same angry stiffness that had descended on her the moment the family had started out for church this morning. The object of her anger was Ellery, on grounds Mary failed to understand, but the reason was of little consequence anyway. Clara, being Clara, spared no one who crossed her path when she was in a mood. Mary was halfway prepared to hear her snap at the minister when she reached the door where he was standing to greet his departing congregation.

"A very fine sermon, Reverend Beech," Clara told him as if she meant it. "I'm glad we were here to hear it. This is my little sister, Mary James, up from Sun Prairie. She's volunteered to be the extra right hand I need this fall."

Volunteered! Mary stifled a gasp of indignation. She would as soon have volunteered to break an arm, and Clara knew it.

"Welcome to Peshtigo, Miss James," the minister said, pressing her gloved hand gravely. "I know Mrs. Cody is going to find your assistance a true blessing. Sun Prairie—that is somewhere near Madison, isn't it?"

"Ten miles northeast of Madison," Clara answered for her. "A long way from here, practically the length of the state away."

Mary wondered if this were meant as a reminder that she was in Clara's territory now, where Clara made the rules. As if Mary needed a reminder.

"Well, we'll try to make you feel at home during your stay with us, Miss James, I'm sure," Mr. Beech said. "It's a pity you have to find us so dusty and dry a place at present. All we can do, though, is keep praying the Lord will break this drought and send us rain soon."

"Yes, sir. It has been a bad year everywhere, I guess, all over Wisconsin," Mary said, mainly to prove to him she did have a voice. Then, because there seemed nothing more to say and because others were crowding behind her, waiting their turn to be greeted, she added, "Thank you."

Mr. Beech gave her hand a dismissing pat, and she descended the wooden steps to the hard-packed earth of the yard. It was of no consequence to her anymore whether it rained soon or not. She could not leave until after Clara's baby was born, and who knew for how many weeks Clara would detain her after that?

Maybe if there had been a decent amount of rain this summer everything would have been different. Pa's worry over his parching crops would not have frayed his temper to where he had refused at last to hear another plea or protest from her and declared it was her duty to go to Clara and that there would be no further debate. Ma had tried to sweeten the pill by saying, "You're remembering her the way things were when you were just a little girl. Now that you and Clara are both grown up, things are bound to be different between you. It's a compliment, really, that she feels she can depend on your help when she is going through such a difficult time."

But Ma was either an impossible optimist or else she did not know her elder daughter very well. Or maybe, like Pa, she was simply worn down by the deluge of letters Clara had written home all summer urging that Mary be sent to her—which was not a compliment of Mary's capability, but merely an act of desperation.

A small hand brushed at Mary's skirt. She looked down to find Netty, a pig-tailed miniature of Clara, fingering a fold of the material.

"You got ashes on you," Netty explained shyly.

"Ashes?" Mary frowned at a dusting of white flecks on the forest green cloth. It looked almost like a powdering of snow, except that the day was far too warm for snowflakes. "Where would I get ashes?"

"From the fires burning in the woods. They're in the air everywhere. It's just something you'll have to learn to live with until we get a good, drenching rain," Clara said, as if she supposed Mary were about to create a fuss. "Ida, you stay close to Mama."

Mary shook off the remaining ashes and said nothing. What was there to say? She knew of the fires in the woods. Every night the sky to the west and north was a red glow that was visible until daylight faded it, and most of the time, except when the wind shifted for a little while, the tang and sting of woodsmoke was in every breath she drew. The steamer that had brought her up the coastline from Green Bay to Peshtigo Harbor had sounded its foghorn time and again because of the smoke cloud that lay thick as fog on the water.

But fires broke out in the woods every fall, Ellery said. It was a thing to be expected and nothing for her to worry about. It was worse this year than usual because of the dry conditions, but for the most part it was only the isolated farms or logging camps in the woods or a lone hunter or wagoner caught in a sudden flare-up of wind and sparks that had cause for alarm. Peshtigo was prepared to withstand any emergency. A wide strip of land between the edge of town and the edge of the forest had been plowed up and picked bare of brush and roots and whatever other debris could feed a flame. Barrels of water stood at every street corner and in nearly every yard, ready to douse a drifting spark the instant it landed. And the Peshtigo Company, whose sawmills, warehouses, and woodenware factory were the heart of the town, owned as modern and up-to-date a fire engine as you could find anywhere.

"Mrs. Cody, good morning!" A slender woman in a velvet bonnet came forward, her hand outstretched. "We missed seeing you before the service. But this, I take it, is your sister Mary?"

"Yes, this is Mary. Mary, our neighbor, Mrs. Collins," Clara said. "We would have been here earlier this morning, but Ellery saw fit to sell our steady old gray yesterday, and we had to wait for him to wear down that mustang bag of tricks to where the beast was settled enough to bring us here."

"How do you do, Mrs. Collins," Mary said quickly, slipping her hand into the offered one in hopes of diverting the talk from this grievance against Ellery.

It had long been Ellery's practice to buy colts and sometimes badly schooled horses at a low price, break them to harness in his spare time, and when he had transformed them into docile, biddable animals, to sell them for a profit. Clara's letters home had often bragged how this kind of enterprise had brought in comfortable additions to the wages he earned as a lathe operator at the woodenware factory. The gray horse had been a business investment, the same as the rest, and its sale was inevitable, a fact which Clara had admitted herself this morning. Yet she was furious about Ellery's having sold it, nonetheless.

Mrs. Collins had a wide, sweet smile that somehow managed to convey sympathy for Clara and warmth for Mary at the same time. "I'm so pleased to meet you, Mary. I daresay your sister won't be working herself into a sick bed every week or so the way she has been doing, now that you're here to keep an eye on her and lend a hand. She has told us such a lot about you that we've been looking forward to your arrival almost as much as she has. Isn't that right, Jewel?"

She turned toward a girl who was standing a little apart, talking to a young man and paying no heed to anything else.

"Jewel, dear, come meet Mrs. Cody's sister, Mary. You, too, Arnold."

Jewel did a graceful half-twirl on her toes that carried her in three steps to Mrs. Collins's side, followed by Arnold. Mary recognized him as the round-faced young man who had been eyeing her in church. Arnold Robinson, his name proved to be; he was "a friend of Jewel's," and lived on his family's farm southwest of town in an area called Lower Sugar Bush. A flash from Jewel's blue eyes and a lift of her hand that almost, not quite, touched his sleeve during the introductions warned that he was also private property.

She was a pretty girl of about Mary's age, or at least, Mary surmised, there were those who would think her pretty, Jewel among them. Her hair was palest blonde, and she wore it in long curls that bobbed against her cheeks and lay in silken perfection on the back of her neck. Her brows and eyelashes were paler yet, giving her face a big-eyed blankness of expression like a painted doll's.

Mary was not deceived by the blankness, however. She was quite aware that behind Jewel's polite smile, Jewel was measuring her, detail by detail, as carefully as she was measuring Jewel. There could be only one "prettiest" girl in the congregation, and each of them was used to enjoying that distinction.

Jewel had the advantage in height of perhaps a full inch, but her waistline, although neat, was no match for Mary's. Neither was her choice of clothes. Where Mary was wearing a shade of green that set off her bright hair and deepened the color of her eyes, Jewel was garbed in a hue of purple the fashion magazines called heliotrope. She could not have selected a more stylish color nor one better calculated to wash out what little natural color she possessed. The effect was to give her more than ever the look of a doll—one whose painted features had been all but worn away by repeated scrubbings.

Mary slanted a smile upward at Arnold, making a small wager with herself that Jewel's judgment concerning the strength of his attachment to her could be proved faulty, too. "So you're farm people. So am I, and I'm afraid I am going to feel dreadfully far from home here in town. I can't imagine where you could put a farm, though, in the midst of all these trees."

Arnold chuckled. "We chop the trees down first, and clear a place, field by field. I expect you'll find the farms hereabouts some different from what you're used to, but I'd be glad to show you around my folks' place any time you're feeling homesick." He bent toward her, earnest and eager. "I know what. Why don't you ride along with us out there this afternoon? That would be fun, wouldn't it, Jewel?"

"That would be a splendid idea, Arnold—if we were going for a ride out to your folks' place. But we have to get busy and learn that duet we're to sing for Minnie Andrews's wedding, don't you remember? We won't have time for much else this afternoon." Jewel gave him a flutter of silken lashes that demonstrated that she was as skilled as Mary in the art of the sweetly persuasive smile.

"Yes, sure . . ." Arnold divided a bemused grin between her and Mary. "But I thought that wedding's not for three weeks yet."

"It's a very complicated song," Jewel said. "We can't afford to waste any chance to practice."

Clara put an end to the discussion. "Mary couldn't go this afternoon, anyway. I can't spare her yet. There'll be plenty of time for jouncing out into the woods on a dusty road after she's settled in here a little more."

So that was how it was to be, Mary reflected; no holidays, no freedom, no fun if Clara had her way. She was hardly surprised. Almost before she had got her trunk unpacked, Clara had begun assigning chores to her, starting with lighting the fire in the stove every morning, which meant Mary had to be up a good half hour ahead of everyone else each day. And yesterday Clara had decided to top the ordinary household jobs by changing the stuffing in all the mattresses, so that the second full day after her arrival, Mary had been obliged to sneeze and itch and cough her way through stacks of fresh oat straw, not to mention tug the filled mattresses back upstairs from the yard where the filling had been done and then remake all the beds from the bottom up. Tomorrow, Clara said, they would tackle whitewashing the parlor walls, the translation of which, if the pattern of these first days held true, was that Clara would stand over her and supervise while Mary did most of the real labor.

The question of whether Clara *could* spare her was beside the point. It was growing ever more clear that Clara had no intention of sparing her, whatever the cause.

Mary tilted her head with a touch of defiance. "Another time, then. Perhaps next Sunday?" she asked Arnold. "I'm going to hold you to your promise, for I'd love to see the farm and to have a ride through the woods."

"I hope you won't find it all too boring," Jewel answered for him. "A ride in the woods sounds so tame compared to the adventures you must have had coming here. Traveling that long way all alone! My goodness!" She gave a pretty little shudder that put her a half step in front of Arnold and between him and Mary. "I'd never have the courage."

The tiny thrill of shock in her voice made courage a synonym for unladylike brazenness.

"Alone? Good heavens!" Mary turned the charge of indelicacy back on her by an arching of eyebrows that expressed even greater shock that Jewel could harbor such a notion. "I traveled with our minister's wife and her son as far as Green Bay, where her mother lives. My brother-in-law met me there, and we took the steamer to Peshtigo the next day. I can't imagine having to manage all that by myself."

She sent a sidelong glance across the yard to where a knot of men were talking under a huge, bare maple. Ellery's fine head and broad shoulders dominated the group like a prince among commoners. Yes, it had been an adventure, being escorted those few hours of the steamer voyage by a man so handsome and capable as Ellery Cody. But she was not about to admit it to anyone.

"I must say, I don't envy you the steamer part," Mrs. Collins said, shaking her head with a little laugh. "I'm no sailor. But the rest of the journey, that long trip by rail—I confess I could be persuaded to do just about anything for the promise of a train ride."

"Mother!" Jewel objected, and rolled her eyes up despairingly at Arnold.

Arnold was scarcely better than a schoolboy in comparison to Ellery—a gawky collection of dangling arms and lanky legs—but he did have a pleasant grin. "By the time Mary's ready to leave us, she'll be able to go home by rail the whole way, the rate they're putting the railroad through. They expect to be running trains clear to Marinette before the year is out, and that's seven miles beyond here." His color deepened again. "I don't mean—well, what I want to say is I hope you'll be staying here a deal longer than it takes to put the railroad through."

"That depends," Mary said, leaving him to judge from her slow smile on what it depended.

"It'll depend in part on whether those wild gangs clearing the right-of-way can get their job finished without burning themselves up and us into the bargain," Clara said tartly. "I've heard it said they're responsible for most of the fires in the woods this year, and I don't doubt it. They're nothing but packs of ruffians imported from Chicago and who-knows-where-else without the least woods sense, and they pile up their slashings and set them afire any time they've a mind to without a care for wind or sparks or anything else."

"I'm glad people have got somebody to blame besides the farmers for once," Arnold said. "We're always careful on our place. My father's never burned off stumps or brush yet except it's a day with no wind, and then he has barrels of water set around just in case."

"Mr. Collins thinks the fires start from campfires—the Indians, and hunters and fishermen—but I'm inclined to believe the culprits are the railroad crews, too." Mrs. Collins shook her head, her eyes widening like Jewel's as she considered the question. "I never thought I'd see anything more rowdy than loggers in town for a spree, but these railroad crews have them beaten. It's getting so a decent woman's not safe on the streets."

"Yes." Jewel's nod sent a pretty shimmer of movement through the curls spread beneath the lower edge of her bonnet. "Just yesterday, when Mama and I were coming out of the cobbler's shop, one of those horrid men actually accosted me. He was so full of liquor he could hardly stand, and he said, 'Why, hello there, you pretty thing,' and tipped his hat. I could have died right on the spot."

Arnold's good-natured face clouded in a scowl. He clenched his fists. "I wish I'd been there."

Mary gathered from the smug look Jewel turned on him, then on her, that a brawl on the street in defense of her honor would have suited Jewel very well if there were no better means of securing Arnold's full attention again.

Clara put a restraining hand on Netty, who was attempting to raise a fuzzy caterpillar from the ground on the end of a stick. "Something like that was bound to happen one of these days. But that's a hazard you run, Jewel, one of the penalties of being pretty."

Both Jewel and her mother laughed and pretended embarrassment at the compliment, or at what they took to be a compliment. Mary was secretly delighted, knowing it was no such thing.

Clara did not set much store by prettiness. Her acid remarks this morning about the time Mary was spending in fluffing her bangs to exactly the right softness would have made that evident enough if it hadn't been before. Clara's auburn hair, her one lovely feature, was pulled back as tightly as pins and combs could hold it, so that not a single softening tendril or wave escaped around her face. To Clara, what was not practical bordered on being sinful, and any personal attention beyond what was necessary to keep oneself tidy and clean was not practical.

"Well, ladies, have you got the world set in order for another week?"

It was Ellery, Tat clinging to his hand and a brown-whiskered man trotting along beside him.

The other man was Mr. Collins, who worked in the woodenware factory with Ellery. He acknowledged Mary's introduction to him with beaming good will. "And now, girls, how about it?" He patted his rounded midsection and chuckled. "I hear my dinner calling. I'll bet it's called Arnold, too. Are you going to lead us home and feed us?"

The group dissolved at once. Arnold Robinson fell into step beside Jewel, who shot Mary a parting smile of complacence over her shoulder. Mary returned the smile without pain, surmising that perhaps another time he might not be so willing to move off—another time when he was not plainly invited to the Collinses' for Sunday dinner.

Clara heaved a sigh and reached for Ida's hand. "All right, Tat, Netty. We're going home, too. Although I'd give a good deal to be able to walk it rather than trust myself again behind that monster mustang."

But of course she was in no condition to cover the half mile or so to home on foot. That had to be obvious to anyone who spared her even a passing glance, despite her tight stays and a skirt too full in front to be fashionable. Mary wondered that she could bear to be seen in public looking so bulky and awkward, much less speak of it aloud within earshot of a dozen people. The baby was due around the middle of November, Ma had said. And to think today was only October 1. It would be six weeks more, at least, before Mary could so much as begin to think of the possibility of really going home.

"Now, Mother . . ." Ellery slipped a hand under Clara's elbow, guiding her forward to where the Codys' light wagon waited among an assortment of other conveyances beside the church. "That mustang has it in him to be the best driving horse I've trained yet. He'll bring more than any of the others when I'm finished with him. You'll see."

"In the meantime, you're willing to risk your family's life and limbs behind a half-trained beast that's a bundle of nerves into the bargain. You can count yourself lucky if the profit you made from poor Dan and every penny you hope for from this one don't go for funeral expenses and doctor bills."

"Or a silk dress for you and a parlor organ, maybe," Ellery said, smiling down at her set face. "I know I promised to hang onto Dan for you as long as you wanted him, but Dorendorfer offered me almost three times what I paid for him. That's not going to happen every day, and he needed the horse right away."

"And there was no real reason for us to keep a safe horse. None at all." Clara jerked her elbow free and walked the remaining yards to the wagon, limping slightly because the coming baby was causing her pain in one hip. "What's one child more or less, anyway, compared to a masterful stroke of business?"

"Now, Mother, I've handled worse than this fellow and survived without a scar. I can manage him." Ellery ran a quick hand down the mustang's black neck. "He's not so bad as you're making out. If I thought he was, you can be sure I wouldn't have let Dan go for ten times the price."

Mary marveled at his patience, for he and Clara had gone through the same arguments twice before on the drive to church. What was done was done, and it had been done in the hope of pleasing Clara, if only she would try to understand that. Why couldn't she just accept the fact and be happy?

Mary gave Ellery a sympathetic smile as he handed her up into the wagon.

Ellery winked at her and grinned through the brown-gold of his beard, scooping Ida up to sit on the back seat beside her. Netty was next. She squeezed close to Mary on the seat to leave room for Tat.

But Tat climbed into the front seat under his own power while Ellery was helping Clara up over the wheel.

"I want to drive, Papa." He anchored himself to the dashboard with one hand and grabbed for the reins with the other.

"Oh, no you don't, young man." Clara caught his arm in mid-reach and pulled him to her. "You sit right here on this seat, and don't you dare make a move toward that animal."

She plopped him down hard beside her. Tat set up an immediate howl. "Papa, I want to drive."

"No, son," Ellery said, taking his place and untying the reins. "This is a man's horse. It takes big hands to manage him."

"I want to. I want to." Tat continued to wail.

"Stanton Randolph Cody, I am warning you," Clara said ominously. "I have a headache already, and if you screech just once more—"

"Well, Mother, let him stand between my knees and watch. Here, Tat, like this." Ellery swung the little boy into position and let him grasp the ends of the reins dangling below Ellery's hands.

Ellery clucked to the mustang, a sound Tat imitated remarkably well, and the wagon was underway. Mary read it as a sign of Ellery's genuine confidence in the horse that he would allow himself to be hampered in such a way.

"We'll drive round by the Ellis' house so Mary can see what the best house in town is like," Ellery said. "Ellis is superintendent for the Peshtigo Company here. He's in charge of everything—sawmills, woodenware factory, sash mill, machine shop, boardinghouse, company store—the works. He drives the prettiest pair of matched bays you've ever seen."

The mustang pricked his ears and pretended to shy as the wagon drew abreast of a slow-moving cart. He stretched his neck forward and would have broken into a run, but Ellery pulled him down to a fast walk before he could start.

"He does do what he's told, doesn't he?" Mary said. She wanted Clara to notice the fact.

"We're getting to know each other. He's got the makings of a really fine horse. Give us a little more time—" He glanced at Clara and glanced away. "There's nothing like a good horse to work with. I learned that lesson inside the first month I was in the infantry back in '61."

Mary leaned forward. "The infantry? I thought you were in the cavalry."

"Right, I was." Ellery laughed. "Christmas of '63, that was. Frank Perry invited me along to spend part of our leave at his folks' place in Sun Prairie. By that time the Wisconsin Fourth Infantry had seen the error of its ways long since. We'd captured and kept so many rebel horses in our campaigns that the War Department officially changed our name from infantry to cavalry. But who would have expected you to remember that visit? You couldn't have been much bigger than Ida."

Mary laughed, too. He had to be joking. "By Christmas of 1863, I was nine years old, going on ten."

"But you never acted your age," Clara said. "You were always the family baby, the little dimpled darling that everybody coddled and catered to."

Mary straightened in indignation. "That's not true!"

"Isn't it?" Clara shifted on the front seat to gaze back at her. Her face, naturally ruddy, was pale, her eyes pink-rimmed above blue pouches. "Pa and Ma had me doing chores and housework when I was Netty's age that you still didn't know how to do when you were twelve. Anything you didn't want to do, you either wheedled Ma and Pa to let you off or else got Grant or Wes to do it for you. They acted as silly over their baby sister almost as they did over a sweetheart."

Outrage whirled a score of retorts through Mary's mind. "I've done my share always. You're the only one who ever wanted more than anyone could possibly give. If you're saying Ma and Pa played favorites, it seems to me that the favors went mostly to you. Why do you think I'm even here?"

"For love of me and the joy of being useful, I have no doubt." A jerk of Clara's shoulders returned her eyes to the horse's rump.

Mary sat staring at the blank, black circle that was the rear of her sister's bonnet. She could not picture a little Clara the size of Netty. Clara had been twelve when Mary was born, and in Mary's recollection, she had never been anything but full grown, cooking as well as Ma, teaching school, imposing her will on those around her too young to put up a telling resistance—which meant Mary mostly, for Grantland and Wesley were close enough to Clara's age to ignore her would-be authority and to go their own ways. Clara possessed a loving spirit underneath her brusqueness, Ma always said, but Mary had yet to see any evidence of it, particularly any directed at herself. But not until this minute had Mary suspected that her sister felt such resentment and bitterness.

"There's the Ellis house." Ellery pointed with his whip, his tone as cheerful as though nothing else had been under discussion.

Mary saw a large house set back from the street among clusters of trees. It was two stories high and, like most Peshtigo dwellings, it was built of wood and painted a creamy white. A neat fence enclosed the big yard, and sawdust-paved walks led to the front door and to outbuildings that peeked here and there from behind the trees.

Trees were everywhere in Peshtigo. Not only did they surround the houses within their fences, they stood in groves in the spaces between the house and the next. And in some places where no houses had yet been built, the block was a veritable woodlot from one cross street to the next. On the other side of the river, the west side, where Ellery and Clara lived, there were more houses and stores and other buildings than the east side boasted, and so more of the trees had been cleared, but there were few patches of sky that could be seen without looking up through a pattern of branches. Beyond the town, the vast northern forest rose like a wall, gigantic white pines towering like church spires, their trunks so massive that each could provide the lumber to build an entire house.

To Mary, accustomed to open fields and rolling prairie land, the sensation was suddenly like being shut into a narrow closet. She felt trapped and helpless and as if she were about to suffocate. How would she ever get through these next few months in Clara's domain?

"Ellis is building a new place," Ellery said, keeping up the pretense that all was well. "There's not much to see of it yet, just a hole in the ground and some uprights. But we'll go over and inspect it one of these days when it's farther along. It will probably put this one to shame."

"Yes. That would be nice," Mary said automatically. Each word was like a small, hard pebble that bruised her throat.

"Why are we turning here?" Clara asked Ellery.

"I thought we would show Mary a piece of the town while

we're out. It's not much farther this way, and dinner will keep till we get there."

"I'm not sure I will. My head is aching, and I want to go home and lie down."

Ellery flicked the reins and set the horse trotting. Whether he was refusing to heed Clara's wishes or speeding up to cover the ground faster and shorten the drive, Mary did not know. Neither did she care.

Is that why she was so determined to get me here? she wondered. So she could prove finally to Ma and Pa how worthless I am? Is she planning to make life so wretched for me that I'll go running home in disgrace?

Mary's hands knotted on each other in her lap. She drew in a slow, long breath of smoke-tainted air, forcing down the sickish flutter that was rising from her stomach. I won't be scared off, she vowed to herself. I can stand up to anything she can throw at me.

"Giddap!" Tat shouted as they rounded another corner, "Giddap!"

"You stop that," Clara told him. "You leave that horse strictly alone. You hear me?"

This street was bringing them into the business section of town. Men in rough work clothes sat on the verandas of the long low buildings or clumped along the wooden sidewalks. Midway down the block, two men in red shirts and heavy boots stood in the middle of the road, their arms laid over each other's shoulders. They were harmonizing, "Tenting tonight, tenting tonight, tenting on the old camp ground," to the applause of half a dozen burly men gathered around them.

"A fine part of town you choose to take a young girl

sightseeing," Clara said. "Saloons and drunken lumberjacks and heaven knows what else. And on the Sabbath, too."

Mary found it hard not to stare at the men, but she lowered her eyes as the wagon swung out to avoid them. She could not tell if they were drunk or not, for she had never seen anyone in that condition, but certainly they sounded a lot happier than she was feeling.

"Are they lumberjacks, Mama?" Netty squirmed on the seat to give them a frank scrutiny. "Where's the nail things on their shoes?"

"Calks," Clara corrected. "If they aren't wearing loggers' boots, more likely they're from the railroad crew, but there's not much to choose between them. Don't stare, Netty, and don't you ever talk to any men like that, not even if they talk to you first."

"Faster, Papa," Tat interrupted, protesting the slow pace the half-blocked street had imposed on the wagon. "Go fast."

"Never mind, son. You let Papa drive. Don't shake the reins," Ellery told him. To Clara he said, "You'll be putting it into her head they're wicked men. They're not. They're just a bunch of fellows letting off steam and high spirits in town after a stint of downright bone-cracking labor in the woods. I've yet to hear of a logger who offered an insult to a decent woman or hurt a child."

Mary waited for Clara to recount the experience of Jewel Collins, but again Tat's voice, growing shriller and more insistent, interrupted: "Faster! Faster! Giddap!"

Before anyone could hinder him, he snatched the whip from its socket and brandished it at the mustang's tail.

"Tat!" Both Ellery and Clara grabbed for him at once.

Tat flung the whip from him and ducked below the dashboard to evade them. The slender whip with its lash of braided leather hit the mustang a glancing blow, rattled sharply against one of the wagon shafts, and somersaulted to the ground.

Snorting, the little horse rose up off its front legs and lunged down on them again, running.

"Whoa!" Ellery yelled, tightening on the reins. "Whoa!"

He might as well have been shouting at the wind. The wagon swayed around another corner and into a street Mary thought was vaguely familiar. She clutched at the seat to steady herself with one hand. Her free arm caught Ida barely in time to save her from being thrown to the floor. "Hang on," she called to Netty. "Hang on!" There was nothing else she could do for the little girl.

Ellery was on his feet, fighting to bring the mustang down. The horse's hoofs kicked up spurts of grayish yellow from the sawdust-paved street. Mary had an impression of tall brick buildings flying by—the Peshtigo Company's buildings—of people shouting, horses neighing, people scrambling to get out of the path.

Next they were on the bridge. The wheels rumbled on the planks. The hoofs struck a wild, hollow thunder. She had a glimpse of glistening water, of great logs floating in a mass above the dam.

Then the wagon was across. The wheels lurched into sawdust once more. Netty lost her grip and tumbled against the seat ahead. Mary was hurled to her knees nearly on top of her. She hugged Ida to her, trying to protect her from the next nasty bump.

She heard herself repeating pointlessly, "Hold on! Hold on!" Ida was wailing like a steam whistle. So was Tat. Netty was whimpering, "Papa! Papa!" Ellery's voice rose above them all, issuing commands the horse refused to heed. Only Clara was silent.

Another wagon was turning at a cross street just ahead. The driver was whipping his team to hurry them out of the way, but he wasn't going to make it. Not at this speed. Not without the two wagons grazing each other and probably overturning. Mary shut her eyes, steeling herself for the crash.

There were shouts, then a violent swerve of the wagon. The rhythm of the hoofbeats changed. So, unbelievably, did the wagon's momentum.

She opened her eyes to see Ellery still standing, straining back on the lines. Beyond him, a man had hold of the mustang's head. The horse was dragging him onward, but the man's weight was also acting as a drag on the mustang. It called for strong arms and nimble footwork to maintain that hold and not be trampled.

Bit by bit the horse was slowing, until at last it halted altogether, sides heaving and head hanging. A cheer went up from a handful of observers on the sidewalks.

"Much obliged, Sig, I must say." Ellery eased up on the reins and sat down.

The man stepped back from the horse and wiped his sleeve across his forehead. "*Ja.* But you were doing pretty good by yourself. If the road had only been clear."

His words rose and fell in a cadence that betrayed the fact

that English was not his first language.

He walked to Clara's side of the wagon, raising a long, beardless face and deep-set dark eyes. He was younger than Mary had supposed. Not more than twenty or twenty-one at the most.

"You all right, Mrs. Cody?"

"Yes, I think so. Or I will be as soon as I get my feet planted on God's good earth again." Clara stood up carefully, holding to the side of the seat for leverage and looking at Ellery. "We are walking the rest of the way home. And none of us will be setting foot in this wagon again until you can provide a beast that is safe enough for Ida to drive."

Ellery cleared his throat as if he were about to say something, but thought better of it and watched, unspeaking, as Sig helped Clara make an awkward descent to the street. Then he lifted the sniffling Tat from where he crouched on the floor and passed him over to Sig, too.

"And you, young man," Clara informed her son, "are going to be taught a lesson you won't forget once your father gets home."

Netty was sobbing, too. A lump the size of a walnut was swelling above her left eye, and a fine trickle of blood was tracing a course down her cheek. She scrambled over the front seat, and on being set down by Sig, ran to bury her face in her mother's skirts.

"Now give me the little one," Sig said, nodding at Ida. "I'll carry her home for you if you like. I'm going that way anyway."

"No need. Mary can carry her. Thank you, Sig. You've

done your share for us already today." Clara paused. "My sister, Mary James. Mary, this is Sigvard Nordquist, our neighbor."

Mary nodded in acknowledgment of the offhand introduction. Sigvard Nordquist did nothing in his turn but stare blankly as he accepted Ida from her.

"Ida is a big girl. She can walk a fair distance on her own feet," Ellery said. His blue eyes searched Mary's face. "What about you? You aren't hurt, are you?"

It was a question Clara had not thought to ask.

Mary set her teeth hard into her lower lip for the length of a breath. "No, I'm fine. Nobody need worry about me."

She gathered her skirts together and moved to climb down on her own. Her knees were shaking under her, and she stood for a moment, steadying herself. It would be dreadful to topple like a sack of flour over the wheel in front of the crowd that was collecting.

Two big hands closed about her waist, and Sigvard Nordquist deposited her on the planks of the sidewalk as lightly as though she weighed no more than Ida.

Mary was less than pleased. She was duly grateful to him for having stopped the runaway, but that did not give him the right to handle her like a bolt of dry goods whose permission for such freedoms need not be requested. Furthermore, his struggle with the mustang had left him smelling strongly of horse sweat and spattered from head to foot with street grime and flecks of dirty sawdust, none of which she cared to have rubbed off on her new green dress or her jacket.

It was Clara glaring at her and at the world in general that saved Sigvard from an icy rebuff. In a rush of defiance, Mary brought the full power of fluttering lashes and dancing dimples into play for him. "Thank you, Mr. Nordquist."

The Norwegian boy—and he was little more than a boy for all his iron muscle and solid frame—went red from the top of his collar to the tips of his ears as she had expected he would.

"*Ja*," he said, "*Ja*" sounding as foolish as he looked.

She knew that he would no doubt be biddable for any whim she might express in his hearing from now on. Let Clara chew that over for a while.

"Come along, children—Tat, Netty, Ida. Mary, are you coming?"

Clara did not stay for a reply, but started off up the sidewalk.

Mary glanced up toward Ellery, wanting to let him know somehow that she was sorry for the way her sister was humiliating him in public. His eyes were on the space between the mustang's ears, one hand stroking the silken fullness of his beard as he pondered a thought which had no room for her.

Mary's triumph went hollow. What did it matter if she made a conquest of Sigvard Nordquist or Arnold Robinson or a score of others like them? It was Clara who would call the tune, only Clara, whatever happened.

"Mary?" Clara and the children were almost to the corner now.

"Yes," Mary said. "I'm coming."

MARY PULLED THE kitchen door shut behind her and stood a moment, savoring the quality of the afternoon. The nip in the air was good against her hot face. Even the ever-present tang of smoke was a welcome change from the stove blacking and strong lye soap she had been smelling all day long.

Well, the stove was polished to Clara's satisfaction at last and the pine floor of the kitchen scrubbed white. Nothing short of perfection suited Clara. She was a slave driver without mercy. Today was no better and no worse than what the whole past week had been.

Mary flexed her arms and shoulders, easing the kinks out of them. Next she was supposed to dig potatoes for supper. She kicked at a drift of dead leaves beside the step. They crumbled to powder under her foot. She crushed a few brittle strays on the step in the same manner, deliberately wasting time. Clara was not feeling well enough to follow her into the garden to supervise. Therefore Clara might just have to wait a while for her potatoes.

The door opened behind her, and Netty emerged into the murky sunlight.

"Best put on a shawl if you're coming out here, you'll catch cold else," Mary warned. She hoped her voice would carry to Clara and prompt her to call Netty back.

It was not that Mary had no liking for the children. On the contrary, she found herself often in sympathy with them under the eagle eye of their mother and her no-nonsense discipline. But they seemed always to be underfoot. Mary could hardly remember what it was like to be free of them, and she was looking forward to half an hour or so alone.

Netty retreated a step. "Mama says the light won't last forever, not to dawdle."

The message delivered, she thrust her thumb into her mouth and slipped indoors as if she would rather not know if there was a reply.

Mary cast a withering glance at the closed door, then bent to pick up a wooden bucket. No wonder Clara maintained there were no hired girls in this area worth their wages. The truth was more likely that she could not get a girl who would submit to her endless demands, not if that girl had a chance of working anywhere else.

But Clara was right about the light, of course. Mary acknowledged that the day was farther spent than she had realized, as she trudged down the path to the woodpile to collect the heavy fork leaning against it. In these parts where great trees towered everywhere, even in the town, and the smoke haze never really cleared, darkness came on fast and early. It would be nice, though, if sometime Clara would not be right about something.

A boat whistle rose in a long, questing moan out on Lake Michigan. It was a steamer up from Chicago or Milwaukee, probably, feeling its way through the smoke fog on Green Bay to Peshtigo Harbor, where it would load up on Peshtigo lumber and wooden goods. The whine of the sawmills and the rumble of machinery wailed a relentless counterpoint to every other sound in town for eleven hours each day. Ellery said she would grow so used to it in time she would not hear it, but her ears were far from achieving that amount of indifference yet.

She set the bucket down beside a shriveled potato plant and gave the fork a half-hearted push into the sandy soil. Suddenly she was gripped by such a yearning for home and for Ma and Pa that she was winking tears from her eyes. At home that whistle would have been from a passing train, and there would be no other sounds but the friendly ones of animals and farm life and the wind on the open fields. At home there were plenty of chores to do, too, but after the work was done there were friends to visit and parties to go to.

She had not even been able to attend Wednesday evening prayer meeting this week because Clara's hip had been too lame for her to want to go. Although Ellery would have escorted Mary as far as the meeting door and would come to walk her home afterward, she had not felt right about cutting into the limited time he had each evening for working with the mustang. Besides, she did not fancy walking solitary and friendless into a room full of strangers where the only person she knew was Jewel Collins. It would be all the advantage Jewel would need to see to it that solitary and friendless was how Mary would remain.

At that, Mary might have been tempted to go alone for the sake of the challenge had she thought Arnold Robinson might be there, but Ellery had said, "I doubt it's going to be much of a meeting this week, anyway. Not many of the young folks from outside of town are likely to come in, the way the roads keep being blocked by fallen trees these last few days. These fires in the brush gather around the base of a tree and gnaw away at it until a spurt of wind pushes it over and you have a road block it takes a crew of men half a morning to clear."

So that was that.

The fork brought up a half dozen potatoes, small and not very promising. She tossed them into the bucket and moved to the next plant. Blackened leaves and withered stems told the tale of recent frosts. Strange that the nights could leave a dusting of frost crystals on pump handles and well curbs for the sun to melt, but still there was no rain. If only it would rain and freshen the air by dousing the fires and clearing the smoke, maybe it would bring life here a step closer to being endurable.

Plop, plop, plop. Three more potatoes went into the bucket. She set her foot on the fork and drove it deeper into the soil in case she had missed any.

A movement near the gate caught her eye. A man stood there watching. No, not a man. That Nordquist boy. Sigvard Nordquist. Such an outlandish name. He worked as a blacksmith in the Peshtigo Company's blacksmith shop, she had learned, and he lived with his widowed aunt in a log house a block down the street from the Codys.

This was not the first time this week she had surprised him simply gazing at her and saying nothing. He had paid them two visits since the day he stopped the runaway, one to ask how everyone was doing after that unnerving experience, and another to consult with Ellery about the mustang's shoes. At least those were the excuses he gave. In point of fact, he had spent most of both occasions staring at Mary, making stupid, stammering answers to remarks directed to him, and smiling vacantly into space when there was no reason whatever for smiling. Mary was beginning to regret the impulse that had prompted her to charm him that first day. He was such a dolt, and becoming a nuisance into the bargain.

"Well?" she demanded over the top of the fork handle.

Sigvard Nordquist's complexion went predictably red. "*Ja*," he said, shifting his weight on his feet. "*Ja*—I was thinking." He labored at each word as if it were a boulder he were lifting. Then in a rush: "Such a big fork for such a little girl."

The observation was punctuated by something very like a chuckle.

Mary was startled by an impossible suspicion. Behind that accent and that bland face, could he be laughing at her?

She resettled her grip on the fork and resumed her digging in earnest. "I believe I'll manage, thank you."

The gate creaked, dry leaves crunched under boot soles, and the fork was taken out of her hands.

She clutched at the handle, outraged. "Here, now! What do you think—"

"Let me. Please. I would like to." The fork bit into the

depths of another hill with an ease that put her struggles to shame.

Well, if he were so fond of digging potatoes, why not let him. He might as well be of some use. It certainly was not a chore she loved dearly enough to fight over.

She stepped back to give him room. Four good-sized potatoes thudded into the bucket and the fork was bringing up a fifth in the time it had taken her to unearth only one.

"Do you do this for every girl you happen to see working?" she asked innocently when the sound of digging and of potatoes bumping one another threatened to become all there was to hear. "Come into the yard, I mean, and do her chores for her?"

The fork dug in twice more while he pondered his answer. "No."

Mary waited, allowing him time to add something like, "Only for the pretty ones." That was what Frank Linden or several of the other boys back home would have said. They knew it was the sort of answer that was expected, just as she knew it was the truth. It was rather like a game they played.

There was a flicker in the glance Sigvard gave her that caused her to think for a moment that he might have an inkling of the game, too. But never had she seen a brain appear to function more slowly than his.

"So, you're particular? You pick and choose?" she prodded. "How do you decide?"

He considered this, turning over a forkful of earth. "When I see that Mrs. Cody will be a long time getting her potatoes otherwise."

The bucket was heaped full now. He swung it off the

ground. "She is a fine woman, Mrs. Cody. She was the first to come help my aunt when my uncle died, first ahead of even the Norwegian ladies."

Mary could readily believe that. Clara was not one to pass up a chance to take charge and issue orders. And if Sigvard were a fair sample of the rest of his family, it was not to be wondered that they were grateful to have someone step in and do their thinking for them.

"I'm sure she was only too happy to do it," Mary said. She nodded at the potatoes. "Why don't you take those in to her yourself?"

She turned from him to examine a row of blackened tomato vines, letting him know that he was dismissed. He was slow to take the hint, but when she said no more and did not look around, he finally scuffed off toward the house.

There was nothing worth salvaging among the tomatoes or anywhere else in the garden at this late date, but if she went indoors right now, Clara would immediately have twenty more chores for her to do. Daylight was fading fast, which meant Ellery would be home soon. It would be pleasant to meet him out here where they could exchange a smile and a few casual words, maybe even visit the mustang together in his shed, before Ellery's attention was absorbed by the clamor of the household that awaited him inside.

"Mary? Mama says bring in some wood when you come. We got to get supper started."

It was Netty, standing beside her as if she had sprung up out of the ground, a pan of chicken feed in her hands. Perhaps she had sprung up, Mary reflected wryly. Clara seemed to have an uncanny ability to divine Mary's intentions and to thwart them. Might she not also be capable of causing her children to materialize on a desired spot at a strategic moment to deliver her messages?

"All right," Mary sighed, but she did not really mind all that much. Ellery deserved a good, hot meal when he got home, and doing her share toward preparing it was one way in which she could help make his life a little more agreeable.

She carried the fork back to the woodpile and filled her arms with sticks of firewood while Netty scattered the feed to the handful of chickens that lived in a coop behind the shed. Netty came running to join her, the pan empty.

"A chicken coughed," she confided, glancing over her shoulder uneasily at where the birds were scratching in the dust for their supper. "The speckled brown one. I didn't know chickens could cough."

"I didn't either," Mary said. "But I should guess this smoky air could give anything a cough."

Her own throat felt as if she had swallowed sand, and she noted that Netty's eyes were pink-rimmed and irritated-looking. She would have to check her own eyes in the mirror. If they were showing the same signs, she would rest them tonight under pads soaked in witch hazel so they would be fresh and sparkling for church tomorrow.

Sigvard opened the door for them and took the wood from Mary. He managed to drop two sticks on the floor in his haste to be useful, leaving a tracery of wood dust and bark crumbs on the newly scrubbed boards.

"I'll tend to the fire," Mary said firmly. "You sit down and finish your doughnuts."

He retreated, blandly grinning, to the table, where a cup

of coffee and a plate of doughnuts, one half-eaten, testified to Clara's hospitality. "But you, won't you have a doughnut, too?" he offered, pushing the plate toward her.

Mary was tempted. One talent Clara did possess was cooking. No one could surpass her at that, and her doughnuts were crisped to perfection on the outside and more perfectly delectable on the inside. Not even Ma could equal them.

There were those, however, who warned that too many greasy foods could spoil a complexion, and Mary had no wish to appear in church tomorrow with an array of red dots gracing her chin. She had observed last week that Jewel Collins's skin was flawless.

"No, thank you. I'm not hungry."

"I am. I will," Tat volunteered, and reached for the plate with both hands.

Clara's hand, still holding a partly peeled potato, intercepted him. "You can have *one* and give one to Netty. And you can each give a piece to Ida."

Sigvard did the honors, bestowing two of the biggest on the children. He touched a finger to the green smudge on Netty's temple. "You got quite a goose egg there even now. Does it hurt?"

Netty giggled and ducked her head. "No." She started to thrust her thumb into her mouth, substituted the doughnut at the last minute, then removed the doughnut, untasted, to tell him, "A chicken coughed at me. The air's too smoky."

"Chickens don't cough," Clara said. "I hope none of them is sick." She leaned forward in her chair and gripped her son as he was about to sidle out of the kitchen, his doughnut intact. She broke off a good third of his doughnut and tucked it into Ida's eager, plump fingers.

Netty hastily shoved a fragment, a much smaller one, of her doughnut into the baby's other hand and escaped into the next room unscathed.

"Well, there is smoke in plenty for everyone, that is sure," Sigvard said to his coffee cup. "And it is hard on animals, some of them. And people, too."

"Your aunt, how is she bearing up?" Clara asked. "This weather isn't easy on a weak heart, I know."

Sigvard shook his head. "I worry about her, but she won't say it hurts. Sometimes I see her put her hand to her heart when she coughs, but it's no use to ask. I think she works too hard, but you'd have to tie her up to make her stop."

"I plan to stop in to see her one of these days," Clara said, as if a visit from her would be sufficient to cause Mrs. Nordquist to mend her ways. Maybe it would be at that, Mary reflected.

Apparently Sigvard thought so, too, for he nodded and smiled. "That would be good for her if you could, Mrs. Cody. She always asks about you, but she hardly ever leaves that wash boiler except on Sundays. That farm she and my uncle used to talk of buying, she thinks she can still save enough pennies to give it to me for a wedding present one day."

Did that mean he had a girl somewhere he was giving serious thought to marrying? Mary was surprised into looking at him, but he was already looking at her, his dark eyes dreamy and pensive.

She picked up the broom and began pointedly sweeping up the mess he had created in front of the woodbox. The sooner he got any notions about her out of his head, the better.

Sigvard hitched himself forward on his chair as though the seat were not quite comfortable. "Well, I think I'd best be going. Thank you for the doughnuts, Mrs. Cody." He finished his coffee in a gulp and got to his feet.

"Thank you for helping with the potatoes. I know Mary appreciates it." Clara sent Mary a glare that permitted no contradiction.

"Of course, I appreciate it." Mary pressed the broom handle to her heart in an excess of earnestness. "You seem always to be on hand at the very moment you're needed, Mr. Nordquist. Even before the moment. I wonder how you do it?"

Sigvard eyed her uncertainly, his smile a trifle bewildered but his blush as ruddy and as predictable as ever. "*Ja*, well . . . Sure."

He took his cap from the corner of the table and backed himself out the door.

Clara hardly waited for the scuff of his footsteps to fade to fix an icy stare on Mary. "I can tell you there is one thing I do *not* appreciate. I do not appreciate seeing a decent, hard-working young man being made a fool of to tickle a spoiled girl's vanity."

"Don't blame me for God's doing. He was a fool long before I met him, and I'm not tickled by it in the least." Mary swept the broom in an angry thrust that sent her pile of wood fragments skittering toward the door. "Anybody with a grain of sense wouldn't keep hanging around where they aren't wanted. I vow, I never invited him."

"Oh, didn't you?" The pan of potatoes clattered onto the stove top. "I may not be the most beautiful woman that ever walked the earth, but I'm not totally stupid. I know what your little tricks are, and I know how you use them. One of these days, though, the world isn't going to roll over and wag its tail happily just because you show your dimples, and then what are you going to do?"

"Well, I won't turn smug and self-righteous, always sitting in judgment on people and being holier than thou. That's a promise." Mary flung the door open and sped her sweepings over the doorstep and into the dust. She hurled back over her shoulder, "And I positively won't come to you in hopes of any sympathy. That's a promise, too."

She remained poised on the doorstep for a minute while the wind lifted her bangs from her hot forehead and swirled past her into the kitchen. A dozen more retorts, long overdue, were seething in her like water in a kettle, ready to burst into jets of scalding steam at Clara's next word.

But Clara said nothing more. She was at the stove, her back as rigid as a slammed door, when Mary came in and restored the broom to its place. Mary did not speak, either, and the preparations for supper went on in a tight-lipped silence that was broken only by the sizzle of frying pork chops and an occasional murmur from Ida, who was feeding particles of doughnut to a clothespin doll and doing her share to strew crumbs and stickiness on the clean floor.

Netty's cry, "Papa! Here comes Papa!" from the front room was a welcome ray of light cutting through the gloom.

Mary's hands rose at once to her hair to smooth it where it should be smooth and fluff it where it should be fluffed.

She caught Clara's grim eye on her, charging vanity, and defiantly ran her fingers twice more through her bangs. It was a temptation to join Tat and Netty in their race to the door, but she contented herself with setting Ida on her feet so that she, too, could toddle to greet Ellery.

The climate of the kitchen changed from angry winter to jubilant summer the instant he entered it. He tossed his hat onto a wall peg, dropped a folded newspaper on the table, rumpled Tat's hair, pulled Netty's pigtail, and swung Ida up off the floor all in the time it took Mary to retie the bow of her apron. His grin approved Mary from head to foot as he put Ida down and stooped to brush a kiss across Clara's cheek.

"How are my big girls tonight?"

"I guess we'll live," Clara said. "Supper'll be ready as soon as you've washed up. Tat, you leave those doughnuts alone. No more."

Tat's arm wavered above the edge of the table, then wilted. He clasped his hands behind his back, his eyes still on the two doughnuts Sigvard had left on the plate.

"Best way to master temptation is to remove it," Ellery said and helped himself to both doughnuts.

"Don't you go spoiling your supper either," Clara warned.

Ellery spoke through a large mouthful: "Not a chance." He winked at Netty and Tat when Clara turned to the stove again, and breaking the second doughnut in two, handed them each half.

Mary feared she would laugh and alert Clara. She shook a finger at Ellery and began clearing the table of Sigvard's plate and coffee cup, and hastily setting out the plates for supper.

"Any interesting news?" she asked as she removed the copy

of the Marinette and Peshtigo *Eagle* from the table to the bench beside the sink.

"In the paper?" Ellery was lathering his hands at the sink. "Well, I only glanced through it, but the editor says the heavy smoke this week has cut down on mosquitoes, if that's what you call interesting. He also says we can breathe easier, never mind the smoke, because most of the combustible material around Peshtigo has already burned up. There'll soon be nothing much left hereabout for the fires to feed on."

Clara set a spoon in the bowl of gravy and carried it to the table. "I believe I could do with a few more mosquitoes and a little less fire if I had the choice. Sigvard told me this afternoon that that farmer's wife died, that one from south of Oconto whose clothes caught fire when she went back into her burning house for something."

"It was a fool thing for her to do. For anybody to do, to run into a burning building once they're safely out of it." Ellery glanced around at his family, taking special note of Tat and Netty, who were watching him as if they hoped he might produce another forbidden treat for them any minute. "If this house ever catches on fire, nobody is going to run back inside it for anything. Is that understood? And nobody is going to stop to hunt for her favorite doll or a picture book or anything. Understand?"

Netty giggled and Tat grinned. "Yes, Papa."

Mary hoped that would be the end of the fire talk. Besides the woman who had died of her burns, there had been reports of two other deaths from the woods fires this week. The charred body of an old man had been found in the remains of his farmhouse and an Indian, his horse, and his wagon had been reduced to ashes on the road. But all three tragedies had happened miles to the south of Peshtigo and in the depths of the woods. It wasn't likely to happen here, not in town. The paper even said so. And if it wasn't likely, why stir queasy little ripples through everyone's stomach by talking about it?

But they were hardly settled at the table before Tat declared in a voice that grew louder as his view of his importance grew: "If fire comes here, I'm going to run fast, fast, FAST."

"No you won't." Clara finished knotting a dish towel bib around Ida's neck and turned to face him. "If there's a fire and we have to leave the house, we will all leave together. Nobody runs ahead. Papa will carry Ida. Tat will take my hand. Netty will take Mary's. Nobody runs ahead."

"Willie Murphy's mama said run." Tat gave her an unwinking stare.

Clara's stare was just as steady. "And I said?"

Small heels banged against the rungs of his chair. "I could run. I'm fast," he offered, his brow wrinkling in a stubborn scowl that was directed gradually downward to his plate while Clara waited. "Take your hand," he said at last.

"And what else?"

Clara made him repeat her instructions in full twice more, then switched her attention to Netty and made her do the same.

Mary pushed a bite of pork chop to and fro through the gravy on her plate without much desire to lift her fork to her mouth. Why couldn't Clara ever let go of a subject once she got started harping on it? Why couldn't she let supper, at least, be a time to relax and be cheerful after a long and wearying day?

"Don't fret, son," Ellery said as he helped himself to a third chop. "If the fire ever gets this far, we'll get away faster than even you can run. We'll all go straight to the wagon and be off like forked lightning."

"I don't doubt that." Sarcasm was heavy in Clara's voice. "Unless by that time we have managed to acquire a horse that is reliable. One taste of taking off like forked lightning is enough for me, thank you."

"Don't be too hasty in your judgment. I've been working that mustang hard this week, and he's come a long way." Ellery laid down his fork and broke a piece of bread to wipe up the last of the gravy on his plate. "He's a changed animal, believe me. Why, even you could drive him now. Or Mary."

"Could I? Are you serious? I'd love to try." Mary's weariness melted from her as if it had never been. Driving the mustang had been the farthest thing from her thoughts until now, but she was aching for a chance to get away from the house, away from Clara, away from tedious chores.

"Would you? Then why not come along with me tonight?" Smiling, Ellery pushed his chair from the table and stood up. "No time like the present. You go do whatever you have to do to get ready, and I'll harness him up."

Mary sprang up, too. "It won't take me a minute. I'll just—"

"No!" Clara cut in.

Mary blinked, and became aware of the cluttered table, her own plate only half-touched, those of the children an unappetizing display of smears and fragments, the serving dishes depleted and soiled. One more of the endless chores that must be done.

"Couldn't the table wait just this once?" she asked. "I'll

take care of it when I get back, all of it. You don't need to lift a finger. I won't be gone so long. Please."

"No."

"Well, now—" Ellery moved a finger across his moustache. "There's no law says we have to set out right away. Later on after the kitchen work's done up will be as good. Better, because there will be less rigs on the streets probably."

Clara flattened both hands on the table and looked up at him and at Mary. "I mean no, Mary is not going to drive that mustang. She is not going to set foot in that wagon while that beast is pulling it. Not while I'm responsible for her safety."

"She'll be as safe in that wagon tonight as she will be tomorrow. Exactly what horse do you think is going to draw you to church tomorrow?" Ellery's brow was suddenly furrowed in the same lines of resistance Tat's had been, only the lines were deeper and the flash of the blue eyes below was hotter.

"It's not going to be that horse. I told you that last week. None of us is riding behind that animal again, I don't care how well he's done this week. I don't trust him."

"It happens that at the moment he's the only horse we have. How do you propose to get to church without him? You're in no condition to walk."

"Then I suppose I shall have to stay home from church until I can walk it comfortably." Clara rose and brought a damp cloth from the sink to wipe Ida's face and sticky hands. "Or until we acquire a horse that's safe for a family."

Ellery shoved his chair under the table and strode to the door. His hand on the knob, he asked, "Where do you expect

I'm going to 'acquire' a horse to your fancy at this hour on a Saturday night?"

"I don't expect you can." Clara untied Ida's bib and set her on the floor. "But then, I didn't expect you would sell old Dan, either, after you'd promised me you'd not."

Ellery's reply was spoken under his breath. It would have been lost, anyway, in the slam of the door as he strode outdoors.

Mary stared after him, then whirled on Clara. "You don't know the first thing about horses. You're scared of them. You always were. How can you set yourself up to judge whether one is safe or not?"

"All I know is that if a horse is ever going to bolt, he'll do it when I'm riding with him. You bet your boots I'm scared of them. I have good cause to be."

Clara was gathering up the plates and scraping the remnants of food off them onto the empty meat platter, ignoring Tat's protest that he hadn't had his pie yet.

Mary remembered hearing the tale of how Clara and a school friend had been riding home with the friend's father when a flapping sheet on a line had startled the team into a wild run. Clara had suffered only a sprained arm and bruises when the buggy overturned, but her friend had been killed. It must have been a terrible experience, to be sure, but it had happened years and years and years ago, long before Mary was even born. All it amounted to now was an excuse for making everyone else miserable.

"I'm not scared of horses," Mary said. "I don't see why I have to pay for your fears. I haven't had a chance to go anywhere or do anything since I got here."

She took the pie from the cupboard and cut two substantial wedges from it, one for Tat and one for Netty. Somehow it seemed a way of declaring herself on Ellery's side—indulging his children as he would himself if he were here.

"A regular prison, isn't it?" Clara clucked her tongue. "Having to do something besides suit your own pleasure once in a while?"

"You don't own me body and soul. I came up here to help out, but I'm not your slave. I have a right to some time of my own, to some enjoyment."

"I have quite enough to occupy me keeping my own body and soul, thank you. I have no desire for yours." Clara moved heavily and painfully across the kitchen to the stove. The lameness the coming baby caused was always more evident in the evening after she had been on her feet most of the day. "But I am responsible for you. I'm the one who would have to answer to Ma and Pa if you came to any harm."

Mary gazed at her without the slightest compassion. "You'll answer to Ma all right when she learns you've forbidden me to go to church."

"Nobody's forbidding you to go to church. You have a perfectly good pair of feet to provide transportation, and it's not that far, not more than three-quarters of a mile. It will give you something to do since you're so desperate for activity."

"I hate walking. Especially in Sunday clothes. I won't do it." Mary clashed a handful of soiled spoons and forks into the skillet that was soaking in the sink.

"I don't blame you. I've seen your Sunday shoes. They

must be a whole size smaller than your everyday ones, and those are none too spacious, I'll warrant."

That was hitting too close to the mark. The narrow, pointed shoes, almost brand-new, were Mary's delight. She loved the dainty, tiny look of them peeping out from under her skirt like doll's feet, but they did pinch.

And because the truth pinched even more, her temper flared higher than ever. She spun around from the sink, drying her hands on her apron and pulling at its strings to untie it. "You want to see me walk? Say one more word, and I'll walk right out that door to the wagon and go with Ellery this very minute."

Clara's neck and shoulders stiffened as if they were lined with whalebone. "Very well, go right ahead. If you think you ought to."

Her eyes blazed at Mary as they had at Tat when he had opposed her, but Mary had no intention of being quelled like Tat. In a fury of action that left no time for weighing consequences, she threw her apron across a chair, snatched a shawl from a peg, and whirled out the door, slamming it after her as emphatically as Ellery.

Ellery was hitching the mustang to the wagon. She heard rather than saw him, for the yard was a sea of darkness interlaced with shadows that were even darker, and he had not troubled to light a lantern.

"Ellery? Wait for me!"

She cut across the garden at a reckless run, almost losing the shawl in her hurry and waking cackles of alarm from the chicken house. The mustang loomed in front of her, a sudden silhouette against the ever-present glow of red that rimmed the horizon.

"Whoa! Easy there," Ellery cautioned, but whether he was speaking to her or in response to the horse's nervous snort, she was not sure.

The next instant she blundered straight into him, going nearly full tilt. He caught her hand to steady her, and held it while she regained her balance and gasped for breath.

"I didn't hurt you, did I?" she asked.

"No," he said, as if giving the possibility careful consideration. "Were you aiming to?"

They both began to laugh.

"I'm going with you," she told him. "I want to see what you've done with the mustang this week."

"You are? Well, what do you know?" His pleasure was evident in the warm tightening of his hand on hers, and Mary felt a thrill of delightful excitement.

He drew her toward the wagon. "How did you get Clara to agree?"

Mary tossed her head. "I didn't. I don't care if she agrees or not."

Ellery halted. "Well, then, I don't know."

"Why? She's not the last word on everything I can think or do. I'm old enough to make some judgments for myself."

Ellery sighed. "She cares a lot what happens to you. You maybe wouldn't believe it, but she was so set up about your coming, she couldn't talk of anything else for weeks."

"I'd certainly have to take it on faith if I did believe it."

He withdrew his hand from hers. She could just distinguish the shake of his head in the dimness. "I don't know what's put her so on edge since you got here. Her time getting close, maybe. Things don't get to her as much if she's feeling good." He sighed again. "I suppose it didn't help any for me to sell old Dan without talking it over first with her. But such a pretty addition to the family as you, I guess I figured it was natural we ought to travel in a little more style."

Mary's disappointment was too keen to be tempered by the compliment. "Just like it seems to Clara that having me here, we oughtn't to travel at all."

"Well—" Ellery swung around to the mustang. Leather creaked as he worked at some adjustment on the harness. "I suppose what she's got in her mind is a time about three years back when I was breaking a pair of colts. They spooked at something in the woods and took us down a rough piece of road for a way before I could get them pulled up. Clara had all she could do to keep the youngsters from being thrown out—Tat was just a baby then and Netty about Ida's size—and the upshot was, well, she lost the youngster that should have come between Tat and Ida."

"I didn't know that. Ma never said." Mary could have bitten her tongue out for admitting that what he had confided as one adult to another Ma had considered too delicate a matter for a younger sister's ears. "But that was three years ago," she amended quickly. "It's got nothing to do with to-night, or you and me."

Ellery's reply was a dry chuckle. "I believe you could be a potent temptation if you ever set your mind to it."

The shadow that was all she could make out of him stepped up into the wagon.

At the touch of the lines, the mustang started. Over the

crunch of the wheels on parched leaves, Ellery's voice came to her: "You can tell her I'll see if Al Phillips has anything in his livery that will serve for tomorrow."

Mary stood where she was as the wagon maneuvered out through the gate and rolled on down the street without her. She wrapped herself closer in the shawl. Crickets were chirping in the dead grass, but there was a nip in the air that promised frost before morning.

The night was extraordinarily still without the whine of the sawmill, shut down now until the start of work early on Monday. Other hoofs and other wheels were audible in other streets. Farther off, an eruption of male laughter suggested that the loggers and railroad men were well into their celebration of the weekend. The saloons were not so many blocks away.

Or it could be a group of Peshtigo's young people off to a party somewhere? It was Saturday night for everyone. Everyone but Mary James.

It was a while before Mary retraced her steps toward the square of yellow light that was the kitchen window. She still could feel no real sympathy for Clara. It was Ellery who needed sympathy.

How could a man like Ellery, so dashing and handsome and full of life, have married a woman like Clara? There had to be more to it than the excuse he sometimes gave: that one cup of Clara's coffee and one slice of her lemon pie had made him hers for life. But what was it?

He deserved so much more. And she, Mary, deserved so much more, too.

Showers of blessing,
Showers of blessing we need.
Mercy drops round us are falling
But for the showers we plead.
There shall be showers of blessing,
Precious revival again,
Over the hills and the valley,
Sound of abundance of rain. . . .

MARY JOINED IN the heartfelt surge of voices that swelled the music to the rafters following Reverend Beech's prayer for an end to the drought, but she kept her eyes fixed on the hymnal she and Clara were obliged to share. The line about the mercy drops rang hollow in her ears. Nothing resembling a mercy drop had fallen in her vicinity for a great long while.

Clara stood rigid as a post beside her. Mary's spine was no more flexible. They had exchanged barely a handful of words since Mary's return to the house last night, and those were only such words as were absolutely necessary. The quarrel between them was still very much alive.

Added to that, Mary was tired. She had slept badly last night. Not because of any sense of guilt, however. It was Clara's part to feel guilty. The fault was all hers—for insisting that Mary come to Peshtigo, for demanding endless drudgery of her, for eternally belittling, complaining, and picking flaws.

No, Mary's conscience was clear, but her throat was scratchy from so much smoke in the air, and the inside of her eyelids persisted in smarting regardless of how often they were bathed in cool water and witch hazel. The effects of the smoke were beginning to show in the children, too. Clara had been up twice in the night to administer horehound syrup to Netty to soothe a fit of coughing. Tat was an unsavory combination this morning of a snuffly nose and self-pitying whines, and Ida was at this moment chewing fretfully on her bonnet ties while digging her fists into her eyes.

Even Ellery was glum. It was plain that he took no pleasure in driving the plodding old plow horse he had brought home last night, and he was in no humor to talk about it or anything else. Mary's try at cheering him with smiles and light talk drew nothing but monosyllables from him and one dry chuckle that changed no detail of his expression. She might as well have tried to liven up the whip socket.

As if all that were not depressing enough, each time she lifted her eyes from her lap or the hymn book, they rested on Arnold Robinson just two pews ahead—on his imperturbably turned back. He had given her such an open, beaming smile when he walked in that she had been almost sure he had braved the hazard of the road to town in part, at least, to see her again. Since then, however, he had not sent another glance in her direction nor, as far as she could tell, another thought. He was sharing the Collinses' pew and Jewel's hymn book, and his head was bent over the page so close to hers that their cheeks were nearly touching. No one appeared to be marking this display with any disapproval, most particularly not Mr. and Mrs. Collins. She could well imagine what comments Clara would have, however, if it were Mary indulging in such a cozy little scene.

"Amen!" resounded from the congregation.

Mary straightened away from Clara and seated herself primly amid the rustle of closing hymnals that was the only sound to break an otherwise eloquent space of silence. Reverend Beech called for a moment of private prayer, then thanked the Almighty for having spared the town thus far from the dangers that surrounded it and reminded Him again of the urgent need of rain.

Mary's gaze clung to her hands folded in her lap for the rest of the service, and it remained demurely downcast through the bustle of ushering the children out of the pew afterward, greeting Reverend Beech at the door, and clutching to save her bonnet from a gust of wind outside. She was resolved to take no notice of Arnold Robinson unless and until he spoke to her first. There were other young men here and about who would be glad to respond to a smile from her even if he were not.

He emerged from the church as he had gone in, among the last and accompanied by the Collinses, Jewel at his side. To

Mary's surprise Jewel waved and sang out, "Good morning, Mr. and Mrs. Cody. Mary, good morning!"

"Good morning," Mary returned automatically, and was further puzzled to have Jewel come smiling toward her as if they were old friends. Arnold was smiling, too, but not at Mary so much as at the whole general area where she stood.

"What do you think of this sky?" Mrs. Collins asked of Clara. "It's so dark I could almost believe we really are on our way to a storm at last."

The sky did look stormy, although in a way Mary had never seen before. A queer, yellow haze hung over everything. Objects only a short distance off—people, horses, trees, wagons, the schoolhouse across from the church—all had the dimmed, smudged appearance of a poor photograph.

"Oh, Mama, no. Not today. I don't want it to rain today." Jewel fluttered her hand as if to ward off stray raindrops, the same hand she had used to wave at Mary—her left hand, Mary realized, on which something not at all like a raindrop glistened.

"A ring!" Mary burst out before she thought. She went on quickly in order not to seem too astonished, "I didn't see that last week, did I? Is it new?"

Mr. Collins chuckled. "New enough to spank."

"Daddy!" Jewel flushed a pretty pink and extended the hand to Mary. "It happened so fast! We didn't really plan it. We were just walking by Mr. Hays's jewelry store yesterday evening, and Arnold said let's go in for the fun of it. We did, and—well, he bought me the ring."

If a trace of triumph, a spark left over from last week's rivalry, were hidden anywhere in this account, it was buried too deep for Mary to detect it. Jewel was radiating a genuine happiness that it was impossible to doubt. And Arnold was grinning down at her with such self-conscious pride that he looked foolish. He might have cast an appreciative eye elsewhere a week ago, but today he belonged securely to Jewel.

"How pretty. Opals are so lovely," Mary said, to mask a twinge of envy she did not understand. "Have you set the date yet?"

Why should she be envious? It was indeed a pretty enough ring, but she had seen rings far prettier. As for Arnold, she had never seriously wanted him. Attracting him had been only a game.

"No date yet," Arnold said, "but we're thinking maybe some time in December. Maybe Jewel's birthday." He glanced at Mrs. Collins, who smiled her approval.

"Well, congratulations," Ellery said, shaking first Arnold's hand and then Mr. Collins's, while Clara inspected the ring in her turn.

"Very pretty, very, very pretty," she said, "but you're so young."

"I'll be eighteen on my birthday. That's not young. I can't stay a little girl forever." Jewel laughed and lifted her eyes to Arnold.

A fresh gust of wind flattened Clara's skirt against her thickened figure and tore the words of her reply from her. It was no great loss, Mary suspected. It was undoubtedly something sour calculated to dampen Jewel's glow. That seemed to be Clara's mission in life: throwing icy water on any pleasure other people found in living.

Couldn't Clara remember how she must have felt the day

Ellery put his ring on her finger? Mary's own recollection of that day was hazy, but it was no tax on her imagination to know how she would have felt in Clara's place. Maybe that was why she envied Jewel: not because Jewel had Arnold but because Jewel's future was settled exactly as Jewel wanted it to be. She was going to spend it with the one person of her choice and with the blessing and approval of everyone else.

Mr. Collins squared his hat, which the wind had knocked askew. "By jing, I'm almost ready myself to believe a storm is brewing. Could be we ought to get started for home or we'll get wet." He grinned at Ellery. "I'd offer to race you, but I saw that firebrand you're driving, and it wouldn't be fair. We're afoot today, you see, and we'd win too easy."

His guffaw was echoed by Arnold and two or three other men standing near by. Ellery responded in kind to the good-natured chaffing that pursued him as he headed for his wagon, but Mary writhed with the humiliation he must be feeling. Ellery Cody, known for his handling of spirited animals, obliged to plod behind a nag that couldn't run even from a wolf pack snapping at his heels. She stepped around Ida, who was toddling off on a course somewhat at an angle to the rest of them. Let Clara see to Ida. Mary hurried to catch up to him.

"Ellery, will you let me try driving home, please? I don't get many chances to practice, and I want to learn."

And if people saw the reins in her hands and him instructing her, the snickerers might have to swallow a few of their grins on the chance that Ellery had selected such a placid animal for a less humbling purpose than to do penance for last week's runaway.

Ellery paused, studying the drooping lines of the livery horse as if he had not seen them before. Mary wondered if he had heard her. She was about to take advantage of a lull in the wind to try again when he turned to her, a twinkle in his blue eyes.

"Why not? I can't remember when I had a pretty girl to do my driving for me. Maybe between the two of us we can keep this charger down to a walk."

Clara offered no objections to the change in seating which put her in back and Mary up front. Tat, however, when he grasped the significance of the new arrangement, discovered a passionate fondness for Mary that would not let him be parted from her side wherever she sat.

"You gonna drive, Mary?" he asked in a mixture of awe and disbelief as with a series of clucks, repeated slapping of the reins, and finally a light touch of the whip, she got the horse underway. "You really gonna drive us?"

It occurred to Mary that he had probably never seen his mother take the reins and probably never would. The sense of showing herself capable of doing something Clara could not do added a dash of exhilaration to the joy of knowing she was helping Ellery.

"Yes, I really am," she told Tat. "And if you're good and listen to your papa, maybe he'll let you drive a little way after we're across the bridge."

"Maybe," Ellery conceded to Tat's immediate demand to have this promise verified. But Ellery's deep chuckle was for Mary. "I guess where Mary is, we can count on finding some brawny Scandihoovian or other close by, panting to rescue her if anything goes wrong."

Mary screwed up her face at him as though she had bitten into a lemon, and together they burst into laughter. No lectures from Ellery on properly appreciating Sigvard Nordquist. It was obvious to him that a gawking, tongue-tied youth who was barely at home in the language when he did speak was no more her style than this shambling nag was Ellery's.

"Behave yourselves," Clara cautioned from behind them. "You'll have everybody looking at us and wondering if you've lost your minds and gone back to your second childhoods."

People were looking at them, Mary realized. Any number of heads were turning to watch the wagon creep by. But most of the faces wore smiles, some tolerant of the merriment, some amused by the poor horse, and some frankly pleased by the spectacle the front seat presented.

Mary stole a downward glance at herself and then at Ellery and smiled, too. They were a handsome couple sitting there together with Tat between them. There was no denying that, even had Mary wanted to. And Tat, his earlier sulks forgotten and his cheeks growing pink from the wind, was as pretty a child as anyone could hope to see. A stranger might easily mistake them for a family—husband, wife, and child; never mind that seventeen was a shade young to be the mother of a four-year-old.

She let her mind slip again to thoughts of what it would be like to be in Clara's place. It could do no one any harm to pretend just for a little while, just until they reached home.

The Collinses and Arnold were starting down a path that cut across lots through a grove of trees as the wagon came up even with them. Jewel was busy working her left glove on over her new ring and contrived not to see them. In the process, she let her handkerchief be torn from her by the wind and with a little cry sent Arnold scrambling through dust and scattering leaves in pursuit. Mrs. Collins, though, smiled and waved, and Mr. Collins, nodding cheerfully, raised his hat.

"Collins won't be that jaunty when the bills commence to come in for that wedding," Ellery said when they were beyond earshot. "They've never refused that girl anything, and she'll cost them a pretty penny this time, I'll bet."

"It's Ellen Collins who'll feel the worst pinch, I'm thinking," Clara said. "She and Jewel have always been so close, more like sisters than a mother and child. A body could almost envy them at times, but I don't know what Ellen will do for company with Jewel gone. She'll be lost. And so will Jewel, without her mother to do for her. I doubt that child has ever had to learn the difference between a saucepan and a stove lid."

That was a peculiar definition of sisterhood, coming from Clara, Mary reflected. If companionship and indulgence were Clara's dream, she might well envy the Collinses, for that was certainly not how she ran her personal affairs. All the same, Mary was not without a touch of complacence at the thought that she outranked Jewel in the field of household skills.

She gave the reins a contented slap which had no effect whatever on the pace of the horse. "Do you really think she'll have a fancy wedding?"

"Fancy as they come," Ellery said. "You wait and see."

"But they said December. I won't be here." It was the most pleasant regret Mary had ever experienced.

"Why won't you be here? Where else would you be?" The wind tossed Clara's question into the front seat like a sharp cinder.

"Home." Mary twisted to aim the answer directly at her so there would be no mistake. "I only promised to stay until after—until you're up again and able to manage on your own."

Clara's square face set into lines of no compromise. "You promised to stay as long as I need you. That's going to be a goodly share of the winter, or I miss my guess, and you'd better start getting used to the idea."

Mary stared at her, then turned back to gaze into the hazy sunshine framed by the horse's dusty ears.

Not to be home for Christmas? To endure unnumbered months more under Clara's dictatorship? She couldn't do it. She would not. She would find a girl who could be hired to take her place. She would feign sickness and have to be sent home. She would enlist Ellery's aid. He would help her break free . . .

She reached for the whip and gave the horse a smart flick across the rump that produced a stamp and a reproachful snort, but no change of the animal's gait. Her pleasure in the drive was gone. She was conscious of the heat in the wind, drying her skin and roughening her complexion. A new sprinkling of grit and ash peppered her with each gust, and the rich green of her dress was rapidly dulling to a grayed moss shade. The glumness of the morning shut down over the interminable ride.

She resolved to get Ellery aside and talk to him the first chance that offered. Dinner was no sooner finished, though, than he put his hat on again and declared: "I'm taking that horse back to Phillips now."

"Me, too," Tat volunteered. He was still full of the triumph of having held the reins by himself for most of the three blocks from the bridge to the house.

Ellery shook his head. "Not this time, son. Your mama wouldn't like it. I'm taking the mustang along so I can give him a long workout this afternoon."

The disappointment on Tat's face was a mirror of what Mary felt on her own behalf. The whole afternoon to wait through until she could make her appeal to Ellery? She didn't want to delay an hour in getting something, anything, done toward getting herself home and away from Clara before Christmas.

Clara's glance flickered from Tat to Ellery as she whipped the dangling ribbon on Netty's pigtail into a passable bow once more. "You can ride as far as the corner if you promise to come right back. But this time let Netty drive."

Netty's hand came up in a gesture of alarm that was given voice by Tat's shrill of indignation. Even Ellery looked dubious.

"Netty doesn't care about driving," he said.

"That's because she's never had the chance." Clara pushed the little girl forward. "Now you go along and do just what Papa tells you. I want to hear all about it when you get back."

Mary, a stack of dirty plates in her hands, swung around to the window and stood watching as the trio crossed the yard and Ellery tied the mustang to the rear of the wagon. She was fighting to keep down her anger at this newest instance of Clara's tyranny, but it overflowed when she saw

Ellery lift Netty onto the wagon seat where Tat had already scrambled under his own power.

"The poor little mite! She's stiff as a board. Don't you have any sympathy for anyone? I should think you could at least understand how scared she is. She's just like you."

"She's not too scared to try a stunt she's seen Tat do. Not if Ellery handles it right." Ellery's chair scraped the floor as Clara shoved it briskly up against the table. "And maybe I don't want Netty to grow up being just like me."

Mary nearly set the plates down to turn and gape at her. Could it be that Clara—she who knew so positively what everyone else ought to do and how they ought to do it—could Clara be conceding that there were areas where she fell somewhat short of perfection herself? And her comment earlier on being almost envious of the closeness between Mrs. Collins and Jewel—could it be that Clara truly did have a more human side to her hidden away, as Ma had said?

Something softened within Mary. With a little encouragement, it might have developed into the first glimmer of real kinship she had ever known for her sister. But she wasn't ready to give up her anger quite yet. It was high time Clara had to acknowledge that she was not all-powerful.

"Well, anyway, Ellery's not going to force her," Mary reported, and squared her shoulders. "Ellery and Tat have got the reins. Netty's down at the other end of the seat, hanging on with both hands."

"That man! I might have known!" Clara swept Ida up from in front of her and deposited her in the rocking chair without pausing in a headlong charge across the kitchen.

Mary halfway expected her to hurtle on out the door in the wake of the departing wagon or to bellow after it from the doorstep. To distract her, Mary clattered her stack of dishes onto the drainboard of the sink, careless of whether any were chipped in the process.

"I should think you'd be glad he's so tenderhearted."

"Tenderhearted! Oh, yes, he can be wonderfully tenderhearted when it's less effort than showing some backbone and standing firm." Clara leaned her shoulder against the door jamb and glared toward the street. She pulled a handkerchief from her apron pocket and mopped at trickles of perspiration running down her face as she retraced her steps to the sink. The promising wind had faded to nothing outside. The heat in the kitchen was ominous and heavy.

"It doesn't bother his tender heart a jot to drive horses that batter and bruise his family time after time and that put the scare of driving into Netty in the first place." She disposed of Ellery's tender heart by jamming the handkerchief back into her pocket hard enough to strain the fabric of her apron.

"I wonder that you ever married such a dolt," Mary agreed, with what she meant to be heavy irony, but the tremor of outrage in her voice spoiled the effect. "You're a fine one to talk about appreciating people—me and that Nordquist boy. You don't begin to appreciate how lucky you are to have a man like Ellery."

"Oh? If you were in my place, then, I presume you would do much better?"

Mary should have been warned by the sudden quiet in Clara's tone, but she let herself hurtle past any thought of caution. "Do you suppose it would be that hard to better you? Your real luck is that I was only nine and not seventeen when he came courting."

"Or else you would have stolen my beau?"

Mary gathered in her breath in a gasp, appalled by the look she saw on Clara's face and by the truth she had just heard herself declare.

Clara's hands moved slowly upward to plant themselves on her broad hips. "And now you are seventeen, aren't you?"

"No! What I mean—I didn't mean—"

Mary's tongue, so recklessly glib an instant ago, stumbled to a halt. She felt the corner of the sink gouging into the muscles of her back as her eyes and Clara's locked in a long and painful stare. Mary could deny from now until her face went blue that she loved Ellery as anything but a brother; Clara would never believe it. Worse, she was not sure that she believed it herself.

"I think it would be best if I write Ma this afternoon," Clara said. "I'll tell her things haven't worked out quite as we expected, and that you'll be coming home soon."

Mary touched a dry tongue to drier lips that all at once had no power to frame an objection. Anger was quenched by a tide of sickness she could taste in her throat. Ten minutes earlier she had thought she would snatch at any excuse to go home. But to be sent home in disgrace, to be cast out for having coveted her own sister's husband . . .

She had to face around to the sink and brace herself against the wooden drainboard with both hands. "Do what you want," she said to the red pump handle. "You will anyhow."

Clara ignored her. She lifted Ida from the chair, told her,

"Now don't you start snuffling. There's nothing for you to snuffle about," and marched off toward the stairs to put her to bed for her nap.

Mustering the shreds of her dignity, Mary flung after her, "I'll write Ma this afternoon, too."

She hoped Clara might hear it as a threat and reconsider, but there was no sign that Clara heard her at all. The words fell like so many pebbles tossed from the edge of an abyss down into utter silence.

Mechanically Mary resumed the task of clearing the table and getting the dishes washed. When the children returned from their ride to the corner—Tat flapping imaginary reins and prancing like a circus pony, Netty twisting her hands in her apron and watching the toes of her shoes scuff past one another—she sent them up to their mother without asking for details.

Later she heard Clara come downstairs and go into the parlor, and she knew, wretchedly, that the letter home was about to get underway. There was nothing for it but to hang up the dish towel and hurry to set her side of the matter down on paper for her parents, too.

She assembled her writing materials on the kitchen table and poised the pencil she had decided to use rather than trouble Clara for a bottle of ink. The letter should have written itself, but it would not. Her first attempt sounded too spiteful, as if she were purposely exaggerating to prove a point. Her second was so defensive that it read like a confession of guilt. Her third was a profusion of words that filled the page without saying anything whatever.

Three times in an hour she rose from her chair and crossed

the room to throw a crumpled sheet of paper into the stove. At the end of the hour, she had still progressed no farther than:

Oct. 8, 1871

Dear Ma and Pa,

Her head was beginning to throb from the afternoon heat. Her hand left a damp smudge wherever it touched the paper. Nothing was going right. She crumpled this last sheet, too, and went upstairs to her room where, if she wanted to, she could cry.

The little room was stifling, and the tepid water in the pitcher on the washstand did nothing to cool her when she splashed it on her face. Well, it was only fitting that she be as miserable outwardly as she was inside. For it was true: if she could have her choice of any man in the world, she would take Ellery Cody without a second's pause. And if anything should ever happen to Clara—

No! Wicked, wicked thought! She sank onto the edge of the bed and pressed her hands to her temples to drive off such a shameful speculation. Clara had every right to despise her. And Ellery . . . but surely Clara would not tell Ellery.

She loosened her dress and her stays and lay down to ease the ache in her head. When she heard the children stirring after their naps, she crossed the hall to their room and got them up, but she didn't go downstairs herself. She stayed hidden in her room until Netty called her from the foot of the stairs that supper was ready.

Clara had put together a cold supper of bread, ham, cheese, pickles, and applesauce. There was no place set at the table for Ellery, Mary realized as she silently took her own chair, and Ellery was nowhere to be seen. Neither was the wagon back in its customary spot in the yard. She felt a surge of relief mixed oddly with disappointment, for she had been dreading having to face him with her knowledge of herself, yet it seemed that his presence, so steadying and tolerant, would make the whole terrible situation less intense somehow.

"Where's Papa?" Tat demanded. It was the question Mary was hoping one of them would ask. Never again must she refer to Ellery in front of Clara.

"Papa sent Sigvard by to say that he and some other men went out west of town to keep sparks from blowing into the marsh and catching fire," Clara said. Her eyes were on the slice of bread she was buttering for Ida. They did not swerve in the slightest toward Mary's side of the table.

Netty lowered a spoon of applesauce from her lips untasted. "Is the marsh on fire?"

"Didn't I just say Papa was out there to see to it the marsh *won't* catch fire? There isn't any fire out there now. It's only that a breeze is stirring, and Papa and his friends want to be there so it can't make trouble."

As if by way of punctuation, a vagrant puff of air drifted flakes of gray ash through the open window. Mary watched them settle onto her piece of ham and found that a convenient excuse to stop pretending to any sort of appetite. She longed to know how late Clara expected Ellery would be, but Clara did not volunteer the information and the children were distracted from the subject by Ida's sudden announcement: "Not like cheese," which she demonstrated by dropping her bread, butter side down, on the floor.

Not a word was spoken between Mary and Clara at the table or afterward. Anything that needed saying they addressed to one or another of the children. When at last the children were put to bed for the night, Clara withdrew to her own bedroom, and Mary was left to occupy herself in whatever solitary fashion she could.

Mary wandered from room to room downstairs, unable to sit still long enough to apply herself to anything. She lit a lamp in the parlor and picked up a book but set it down again without even reading the title. She considered making another try at writing home, but her thoughts were in no better order this evening than they had been in the afternoon. She wished Ellery would come home. She yearned for a chance to listen to him and look at him and to bask in the delight of being near him, uncensured, just once more before Clara shamed her in front of everyone.

Without consciously planning to be there, Mary found herself out of doors and following the path to the gate. The air in the yard was no more refreshing than that of the parlor. If anything, the unseasonal heat of the day had risen several degrees with the coming of darkness. But then, it wasn't actually dark. The ever-present fireglow that rimmed the northwestern horizon was brighter than ever tonight.

The wind was rising, too. A gust lifted her bangs from her damp forehead and dried her skin like a blast from an oven. A second fierce burst ballooned her skirt and threatened to sway her off her feet. Linking an arm around the gatepost for support, she stared upward where a strange commotion of shrills and twitters was passing above the trees. Dozens of birds, flocks of them, were flitting and darting and wheeling overhead, disturbed perhaps by the unnatural light or the heat, or perhaps by a sense of storm about to break.

A prickle of foreboding stirred Mary's scalp. If the weather signs truly were pointing to that long-delayed storm, it would be a bad one when it came. And where was Ellery?

She peered into the half-darkness of the street toward the sound of running hoofs. They were not the mustang's hoofs, of course; they were too light and no wagon rattled behind them.

But she was not prepared for the animal that did emerge from the shadows and flash by her at top speed. It was a deer, a buck with a splendid rack of antlers. Before she could blink in surprise, another, smaller buck flew by, and in its wake sped a doe, all of them fleeing in the same direction: straight down the middle of the street toward the heart of town, toward the river.

Nothing was in pursuit of them—nothing that Mary could see. She had to shield her eyes behind her hand against the searing heat of the wind as she squinted back along the way they had come. Was that thunder off in the distance, that low, prolonged rumble? Yes, there was a flash of lightning above the black wall of the woods.

But no, not lightning. In an instant the flash became a tree, one of the towering pines of the forest. Its every twig and limb was picked out in tongues of fire. Two more black spires on the outskirts of town erupted into shafts of flame. In the moment it took Mary to collect her wits and run to the house, the darkness paled to a thinning twilight. The whistle on the woodenware factory began to shrill.

Clara was calling her from the head of the stairs. "Mary? Are you down there? Where are you?"

"Here!" Mary raced up the stairs.

"Hurry. Help me get the children up. You'll have to carry Ida. I don't believe I can, and cover any ground. Be sure to get her shoes on her."

Mary nodded, understanding, but not wanting to accept what she understood. "What are we going to do?"

"We're going across the river to the east side of town." Clara was tying on a bonnet as she spoke. "Now hurry. We haven't time to dawdle."

"But what about Ellery?" Mary bit her tongue to stop the question, but too late. It was out.

Clara did not pause to take offense. "We can't wait for him. He'll know where to look if we aren't here." She opened the door to the children's room. "Bring the quilt off your bed. And you can wrap Ida in that wool shawl that hangs over the foot of her crib."

An urgent jerk of the bonneted head sent Mary scurrying into her bedroom for the quilt. She tore open the neatly made bed and dragged the heavy quilt free.

Then suddenly she stood transfixed by the sight framed in her west window. No longer were individual trees ablaze here and there in the woods. The forest itself had vanished. In its place was a solid mass of flame, twisting, bulging, leaping not half a mile away.

The rumble she had thought was distant thunder had swollen in these few minutes to an engulfing roar. It was not thunder. It was wind, fire-breathing wind.

Somewhere a bell began pealing a frantic alarm. Its clang restored to her the power to move. Wadding the quilt up in her arms and stumbling over its trailing ends, she ran to fetch Ida.

CLARA LED THE way down the stairs and out through the kitchen. Tat clutched a corner of the quilt she carried and Netty clung to her by a handful of her skirt. Mary brought up the rear, her own quilt bundled in one arm and her other arm guiding Ida's steps ahead of her.

Outside the door, Clara pulled Mary's quilt from her and plunged it into the barrel of water that stood as a fire protection beside the step. She thrust it back into Mary's arms, dripping and sodden.

"Drape it around you, Indian style," she directed above the roar of the wind.

Mary obeyed, and felt at once a degree of relief from the skin-searing heat of the air. She had not thought to question what the quilts were for. She had only done as she was told. Her mind seemed to have gone numb.

"Come on. Hurry." Clara doused her own quilt and flung

it over her shoulders, spreading her arms under it to gather in Tat and Netty like chicks under the wings of a mother hen.

"Where's Papa?" Tat cried. "Where's our wagon?"

The wagon, yes. They were supposed to leave in the wagon if the fire got out of hand, Mary remembered. She cast a bewildered glance around the yard as if she expected the wagon to materialize because they needed it. But the wagon, the mustang, and Ellery were not there. Only billows of smoke and a reddish light as bright as day and tongues of flame leaping against the sky to the west.

"Papa will find us later," Clara said. "Right now we have to manage for ourselves."

Mary picked Ida up, sheltering her the best she could under the quilt, and followed the others down the path to the gate. There, she turned for a look behind her at the house.

"The lamps!" she called to Clara. "We left them burning."

She started back toward the yellow glow showing through the windows, but Clara's voice, shrill against the wind, stopped her. "Forget the lamps. It doesn't matter."

It didn't matter that wicks alight in kerosene were to be left unattended in an empty house? But that was dangerous. The whole house could go up in—

Suddenly Mary realized as she had not before that the sheets of flame rolling forward on the wind were real. Nothing was going to quench them. Nothing that stood in their path was going to be spared. She bunched Ida up more securely in her arms and began to run after Clara and the children.

Other people were swarming into the street, men, women,

children of all sizes, but Mary heard scarcely any voices. No one shouted advice. No one screamed a question. It would have been difficult for them to make themselves heard above the noise of the wind if they did. Besides, no one had breath to waste on speech. The smoke was so thick that just dragging enough air into the lungs to keep on running was a chore, and everyone was running, staggering, pushing, jostling, running eastward toward the river.

Added to the unbroken roaring of the wind and the wild clanging of the church bell was another sound now: the crackling of flames. Mary did not look behind her. She did not even think of doing it. She had only one thought, and that was to keep close to Clara and to keep moving.

Ashes were raining down from the sky like snow. Something struck her on the shoulder and drove a hot pain into her neck just below her ear. She freed a hand to brush the thing away. It was a glowing ember. She beat the flat of her hand against the charred hole it had eaten into the quilt and was astonished to find that the quilt was nearly dry already.

A man in a nightshirt was trying to back a horse between the shafts of a cart in the yard of one house. A young woman clad in a nightgown and a shawl ran from the house as if to get into the cart. Her hair hung down her back in two thick plaits, and she carried a shawl-wrapped baby in her arms. A toddler about Ida's size was holding to her gown. Just as they reached the cart, a tree in the yard burst into flame from top to bottom. The horse reared and broke away from the man. The man let it go without a second glance. He swept up the toddler into his arms, and he and his wife ran into the street, all but knocking Mary off her feet in their haste to escape.

Mary was having trouble staying on her feet, anyway. The wind buffeted her from behind with the solid force of water racing through rapids. Ida was no small burden, and the heavy quilt was awkward even draped over Mary's shoulders. It kept filling and flapping and propelling her onward willy-nilly like a rudderless sail. Once she was staggered hard against the trunk of a tree, and a second time she caught at a picket of a fence barely an instant before she would have been hurled down on her face.

The air was full of flying grains of sand that stung. She had to fight to hold her head up enough to see where she was going. Clara and the other children were a yard or two ahead of her. Mostly she fixed her eyes on the brown and white quilt that enclosed them and followed that without looking elsewhere.

They gained the end of the street at last and turned north at the corner, toward French Street, the street that led across the bridge. The wind exploded at them from an angle. They were engulfed in a swirl of smoke so thick that Clara's figure was blotted from Mary's view. Smoke poured down Mary's throat, filling her lungs and choking her. Ida twisted in her arms in a spasm of coughing. Mary struggled for breath, but there was none. The next thing she knew, she was on her knees, her nose an inch from the planks of the sidewalk, and Ida was squirming beneath her.

She had no notion of how long they crouched there. It might have been minutes, or it could have been only seconds. The air close to the ground was still breathable. She gulped it in until she was strong enough to lift Ida again and scramble to her feet.

Clara was lying on the sidewalk, too, but she was making no move to get up. Mary ran to her and stopped beside her.

"Clara! Clara!"

It never entered her head to wonder why she should feel panic at the thought of losing this sister she had detested an hour ago.

Clara raised her head, then, gripping Mary's hand for support, hoisted herself to her feet. Coughing and sobbing, Netty wriggled from under the collapsed quilt.

"Where's Tat?" Clara asked between short gasps for breath.

They both saw him at once. He was huddled in the sawdust on the road, his arms over his head as if to ward off a blow.

"I'll get him," Mary shouted. "You go on."

She darted into the street and dragged him upright by his collar. There was no time to be gentle. He hit at her and wrestled to get loose as if he did not recognize who she was, but there was a strength in her hand and arm she had never known she possessed.

As she hauled him up onto the walk, a buggy hurtled by. The driver was laying on his whip, lashing his team to a gallop and paying no heed to anyone or anything unlucky enough to be in his path.

A scream pierced the uproar of the wind: "Help! I'm burning!"

From the tail of her eye, Mary glimpsed a woman flailing her hands against her head. Her hair was a halo of flame.

None of the people hurrying along the crowded walk or in the road stopped to help her. They swerved around her and past her and kept on going.

Mary did not stop, either. She clamped Tat's wrist in her

fingers and tugged him forward. "Run!"

As she spoke, a blazing shingle spiraled through the air and landed on the road at the spot where Tat had been crouching. The sawdust exploded into flame.

Clara and Netty and the brown and white quilt were only steps ahead of Mary, but somehow Mary could not seem to catch up to them. She felt trapped in the sort of nightmare where the faster she moved her feet, the slower her pace became. Two young boys, running like deer, pushed past her and crowded in behind Clara. Tat, frantic at seeing his mother getting farther away, jerked and pulled, trying to break free of Mary's grip. Someone jostled her roughly, and she was staggered to the very edge of the walk. In the moment it cost her to retain her balance, she loosened her hold on Tat. Swift as a minnow, he wriggled out of her fingers and was gone.

She shouted to him and doubled her efforts to run, but she was hampered by Ida's weight and by the quilt, and Tat was weaving in and out among people with a single-minded determination nothing could stop. He reached the brown and white quilt. Mary saw him grab for it and appear to vanish from sight in its folds.

A cow blundered out through an open gate and paused in front of her to bellow its distress. Mary dodged around in back of it as it lumbered on into the road, but the delay was enough for her to lose sight of Clara. As she came to French Street at last and turned toward the river, she thought she saw Clara's quilt billowing onward in the next block, but she was not sure.

French Street was seething with carts, wagons, and buggies, as well as people on foot. Little tongues of flame were licking up through the planks of the sidewalk. Twice Mary had to veer sharply to save her trailing skirt from brushing them, and once she had to stop and set Ida down for a few precious seconds while she beat out sparks along the braid on her hem. Then she snatched the baby up again and ran on and walked on and ran some more.

A man crumpled in front of her. He fell to the ground, face down, and did not get up again. In a strange way, Mary envied him. Her lungs were bursting. She could not get enough air into them no matter how hard she panted, and the air she did draw in burned as if it, too, were on fire. Ida was clutching her around the neck, half-choking her. She wondered how soon it would be before she and Ida sank down and stayed where they were.

A wagon careened out of the side street ahead. It swung out to pass a buggy that was racing in the same direction, but the angle was too short. Wagon and buggy wheels clashed, locked, and pulled apart. The buggy wheel was wrenched from its axle. The buggy pitched over on its side, spilling a man and two women and several children into the dust. Mary did not stay to see how they saved themselves or if they did. There was nothing she could do for them. Nothing she could do for anyone. Perhaps not even for herself and Ida.

Head bent and the quilt pulled over it for what protection it could give against the flying sand and embers, she ran on, hardly seeing where she was going. Wind and heat had narrowed her eyes to little more than slits. In the turmoil of neighing horses, lowing cattle, booming wind, and crackling flames, she had but one thought: to get to the river.

Her toe struck something soft and yet unyielding. She

lurched forward onto one knee and knelt there, panting and collecting her strength before she looked to see what had tripped her.

It was the body of a little boy. He was lying at the edge of the walk as if he were asleep, his face in his folded arms.

For one heart-twisting moment she thought he was Tat. In that same moment she knew he must be dead. Still, she reached for his arm as if she could rouse him and urge him on. His head rolled slightly, revealing more of his face in the glaring light of the fire. He was a child she had never seen before.

There was no visible mark of fire on the little boy. Smoke or heat or lack of air must have snuffed out his life.

As she staggered up, bundling herself and the whimpering Ida closer in the brittle-dry quilt, a spark lit on the little boy's stocking. The wool began to char. Without thinking, Mary stooped and smothered the spark with her hand as if it were somehow important to keep the small body from further harm.

The gesture was senseless, of course. The flannel covering his shoulder was already smoldering from a second spark, and a third sent up a slim curl of flame from a tumbled strand of blond hair.

For the first time, Mary cast a glance backward along he way she had come. The sky was one enormous blaze. Great sheets of flame rose, crested, and rolled over one another like storm-tossed waves.

A huge balloon of fire spun up from the tallest crest and sailed in an arc the width of the street less than a block away. It landed on a house on the opposite side. The entire house burst into flames with a bang. Clapboards and walls thinned and vanished so swiftly that Mary glimpsed the interior of rooms—a bed and chest of drawers upstairs, sideboard and dining table in the room below. Then there was nothing to see but the swirling fire.

Once more Mary was running. She was in the road now. The sidewalks were almost completely ablaze. Patches of the road sawdust were smoldering, too, and there was a risk of being trampled by panicking horses or run down by a fear-blinded driver. But the bridge was only half a block away.

She would not try for the bridge itself. The nearer she drew to it, the better she could see through rifts in the smoke that the bridge was jammed with vehicles and animals straining to cross. Crossing now would be too slow, if not impossible.

She decided she would cut off to the side when she got there and find her way down to the river here on the west bank. The river was wide. The fire would stop at its edge. It would have to. There was no farther it could go.

A young woman darted past her, running lighter and faster than Mary and her hampering burden could. Long flaxen curls whipped in the wind. Her summery cotton skirt billowed.

She was only two or three yards beyond Mary when a burning tree limb plummeted into the center of the street. A shower of sparks danced in the air above it like the tail of a comet. With a suddenness too swift to grasp, the young woman was ablaze everywhere at once—her hair, her sleeves, her skirt.

She halted and turned around. Her wide, blue eyes, more

bewildered than frightened, met Mary's and locked for a second in startled recognition. She was Jewel Collins.

Jewel raised her hands in what might have been supplication or merely a dazed effort to beat out the flames. The light caught the glimmer of the opal on her left hand before she wilted to the ground in an unresisting heap and the consuming fire mercifully hid her from view.

Deep within Mary a voice was crying, "No! No! Please, God, no." But it was muffled in layers of numbness that dulled her senses to everything but the pressure to struggle on.

She was sobbing as she ran, sobbing for breath, sobbing from fear, dry sobs that hurt her chest and stung her eyes without producing tears. She couldn't stay on this side of the river. Not any more. Nothing could possibly survive on this side of the river. The terrible tide surging at her heels might well devour the very riverbank.

But the bridge itself was on fire. Flames were flickering here and there along the supports, and the heavy timbers were charring under the feet and wheels and hoofs fighting their way toward the east side. Mary thrust into the crowd, inserting a shoulder into a tiny space between two men and forcing herself through, shoving aside a cow that stood bawling and shaking its head at the tumult, jabbing out an elbow and delivering a push to a woman who first struck at her to get by.

There was no chance of running here. What progress Mary made was in inches, and sometimes a sway of the crowd sent her stumbling backward a step or two. A cart had managed to get itself wedged sidewise between two wagons, thus blocking half the bridge. Up ahead, a frightened horse was rearing, its lifted hoofs menacing everyone within range. Incredibly, people and vehicles from the east side of the town were battling to get across the bridge to the west side, like crazed horses racing from safety into a burning barn.

A burly man half-carrying, half-dragging a plump, wheezing woman, shouldered Mary from his path without even seeing her. She found herself pressed up against the bridge rail by the surge of people pushing on behind him. The rail was so hot she could feel it through the thickness of her quilt.

An impulse to climb onto the rail and jump into the river right here flitted through her mind. She could not swim, and the river was deep at this point because of the dam, but if she and Ida had to die, wouldn't drowning be less horrible than burning up? Besides, the water below was full of drifting logs. If she could catch hold of one of those . . .

But she was pinned too tightly against the rail to stir a muscle toward climbing it. When another eddy of movement in the throng eased the crush, the movement of so many bodies tore her from the rail and swept her onward with them.

She was scarcely aware of the difference when her feet finally left the planks of the bridge and touched the rutted surface of the road beyond. Panicked people still jarred and jostled her from every quarter. The force of the wind was as fierce as ever. Blazing embers continued to rain down as if the barrier of the river did not exist.

With a sudden, terrifying clarity, she realized why the east side people had been driving against the current of refugees on the bridge. There was to be no escape from the fire on this side of the river, either. In the lumber yard to her left, trickles of flame were snaking along the ground, feasting on shavings and wood chips, while other trickles were climbing up the mounds of sawdust from the bottom and spreading downward from the top. The solid brick walls of the sash factory, the Peshtigo Company store, and the company boardinghouse rose somewhere to her right, but the sidewalk that would lead her there was even now bursting here and there into flame, and the street was a jumble of animals and conveyances, some of them abandoned by their drivers and the traces cut to let the horses seek their own salvation.

Mary swung in first one direction, then the other. If only she could discover Clara in the midst of these milling people. Clara must have made it to this side of the river by now. And Clara would have her wits about her. She would know exactly what to do.

Ida let out a shriek of pain and jerked her arm away from its hold on Mary's neck so suddenly that Mary nearly dropped her. The quilt was on fire. So was the sleeve of Ida's nightdress.

Mary threw the quilt off and pulled the wool shawl from Ida that Clara had directed her to wrap around the baby. She swathed the burning sleeve in the folds of closely woven wool, and the little flame died out. Without pausing to think, she stamped out the larger flames that were in possession of a corner of the quilt. She hardly felt the sharp heat through the soles of her shoes or the burns the sleeve had delivered to her hands.

It was all over in a moment. She lifted Ida against her shoulder again and gathered up the quilt. They both had become a part of her during this endless flight that seemed to have been going on forever. They were all the reality that remained to her in this nightmare to cling to.

But somewhere in that moment she had lost her bearings. Where was the bridge? Which way was the surest route down to the water? Smoke and a peppering of sand blinded her when she raised her head to look. She saw nothing but the red glare of fire on every hand and the murky shapes of buildings she could not identify.

A pair of arms reached out of the haze to tug at Ida. "I'll carry the baby for you," said a man's voice too roughened by smoke and coughing to be recognizable.

"No!" Mary was faintly surprised to hear her own voice as little better than a croak, but she hugged Ida to her the tighter. To be separated from her was unthinkable.

"All right. But you come. This way." A firm hand grasped her elbow and propelled her forward.

He was Sigvard, Mary realized belatedly. She was not astonished, but merely relieved. Any voice of authority would have been welcome at this stage.

She let herself be guided by him past a smoldering buggy, around the scattered bricks of a wind-smashed chimney, through a narrow lane between two flaming walls. He was guiding another person, too, a heavy, stoop-shouldered woman whose breath came in loud rasps. Every few steps, she faltered and stopped, but Sigvard kept murmuring to her words that were unintelligible to Mary but whose tone was coaxing and encouraging, and the woman would struggle on again for several yards more.

Mary guessed that the woman must be Mrs. Nordquist, Sigvard's ailing aunt. She had a frantic desire to catch the older woman by the hand and drag her on regardless of whether the woman's heart could stand it or not. None of them would be saved unless they hurried. Yet Sigvard, who with his long legs, could easily have outdistanced his aunt and Mary both, stayed by them and stuck to their halting pace as if he had no doubt but that they would have time enough.

Then they were rounding the end of a pile of smoldering green planks, and there, straight ahead, lay the river. At last Mrs. Nordquist did break into a heavy-footed run.

"Pa, wait! Pa! Ma! Granny!" The cry, a child's voice, came from behind them. "Wait for me!

A boy of about ten dodged past Mary and whirled in front of her to catch hold of Sigvard's arm. Dismay loosened his small face as he looked up at Sigvard, next at Mary and at Mrs. Nordquist.

"You ain't—" His hand dropped from Sigvard's arm. His voice thinned upward. "Where's my Pa? Pa—!"

He sped away from them and away from the river, blundering in a zigzag course back toward the fiery street, calling as he went: "Pa! Ma! Mama!"

"No, *lillivun!* No!" Mrs. Nordquist turned to cry after him.

Sigvard's outflung arm turned her to the river again. "Keep going. Hurry."

He planted a hand between her shoulders and one between Mary's and gave a push that sent them into a stumbling run.

Mary needed no further urging. Her hand had somehow become linked in Mrs. Nordquist's, and this time she did drag the older woman forward until they stood chest deep in the water.

The last she saw of Sigvard, he was sprinting in the opposite direction in pursuit of the lost little boy.

MARY PRESSED HER hand over Ida's nose and mouth, drew as deep a breath as she could herself, and ducked below the surface of the water. She could not stay submerged for long. Ida was too young to understand about holding her breath, and she went into a fit of kicks and struggles each time the water swept over her head.

Besides, the river was incredibly cold. Its chill ate into the bones of Mary's ankles and legs and sent shudders through her that set her teeth to chattering.

Yet when she straightened her knees to bring her head and shoulders above the surface, it was like rising into the center of an oven. The drenched quilt that she and Mrs. Nordquist were sharing to protect their heads actually steamed as if it were being ironed. In a matter of minutes, though, it would be so dried out again that they would have to duck themselves once more to keep it from scorching.

"You swim?" Mrs. Nordquist had asked after the first time Mary had dipped herself and Ida.

Mary had shaken her head, not wanting to waste breath that was growing ever more precious between the smoke-filled air and the water.

"*Ja*, me neither," Mrs. Nordquist had said. "We hold to each other."

With that, she had linked her arm through Mary's, and when the heat grew intolerable, they bobbed down beneath the water together.

Mary was glad to have her as an anchor. The footing provided by the river bottom was none too secure, and the tug of the current could easily drag an unwary person off balance and into dangerous depths. Some people were already adrift in midstream, either by accident or on purpose. They were clinging to logs to keep themselves afloat but that was no simple task, for the logs rolled and bucked in the water like living things.

Mary was glad, too, to have Mrs. Nordquist as a companion. It made her feel less as though she had been cut loose from all her ties and left to fend for herself and Ida totally on her own. For all her shortness of breath, Mrs. Nordquist was solid on her feet and almost as unshakable in her manner of facing the horrors all around. She kept scanning the shoreline, watching for Sigvard to return, as if she had every confidence that he would.

"He knows we are here," she said. "He will find us."

Mary squinted toward the shore, too, searching the soot-streaked, open-mouthed faces for him or Clara or Ellery—for anyone she could lay claim to, but without a real hope of seeing them. And in the end, would it truly matter if they were there or not?

The hot, smoke-saturated air was growing ever more impossible to breathe. Her mouth was open, her tongue stretched out like everyone else's, agonizing for breath.

Not a house, a tree, a shape of any sort could be seen on the west side of the river. Everything was swallowed in a mass of flames that billowed outward over the river. The clamor of the church bells was no more. She could not remember when it had ceased.

The bridge was ablaze from end to end. It was no longer an escape route but a death trap for those still striving to cross it. On the east bank the scattered fires were merging into one another, becoming a single sweep of flame.

"It's the end of the world. God's judgment is on us," a woman near her was moaning. "We're all going to die."

Mary listened to the rasp and cough of Ida's breath and of her own. She glanced up into the light that should have been black night sky. Jewel Collins's face gazed back at her from the glare, her features fixed forever in the mute horror they had last worn. God's judgment and the end of the world, yes. How could this night be anything else?

Mary wished ardently she had been a better person throughout her seventeen years. She would answer now for her wicked wish that Clara did not stand between her and Ellery. Payment would soon be exacted from her in full for her temper, her pride, her willfulness—

A tremor shifted the sand under her feet. She thought she felt a quiver travel through the water. There was a rumble different from the noise of the wind and the fire.

The brick walls of the woodenware factory just a little way upstream opened upward and outward. Flame and smoke exploded from every crevice and crack. Wooden tubs, pails, buckets, boards rocketed into the sky—all of them burning. Water splashed and steam hissed as they began to fall into the river.

"Down!" Mrs. Nordquist shouted in Mary's ear. She leaned her full weight on Mary's arm, and Mary plunged with her below the surface.

The end of the world, the end of the world, beat in Mary's brain as she crouched on the river bottom. The end for all of them. This was it, and she didn't care. It was all so terrible, why couldn't she die right now and have to endure no more?

But her body refused to hear her. It began clamoring for air until her knees unbent in spite of her and she was thrust up into the heat and smoke once more, pulling Mrs. Nordquist with her.

Blazing litter floated on the river. The factory, the warehouses, the mill, everything up and down the river was gone. Like the west bank, the east bank was one endless expanse of flame that hid whatever might lie beyond. If possible, the heat was more intense than ever. People who had been huddled in the shallows were moving here and there toward deeper water that offered more protection.

But they were alive. Everywhere she looked, there were heads and shoulders of people still clinging to life. Mary herself was alive. And Ida, gasping and spitting out water as Mary tilted her over her arm and patted her back, and Mrs. Nordquist, wheezing as if she had just run half a mile—they were alive.

Mary felt a tug on the water-logged quilt where it lay half-under the water behind her. Mrs. Nordquist had lost her grip on it completely in the shock of the explosion, and it had slid from Mary's shoulders, but she had managed to keep a corner of it wrapped around Ida. She reached for the trailing edge to draw it up over her bobbing head once more. Another tug, stronger than the first, jerked it from her fingers.

Mary twisted to see behind her. A man had hold of the quilt's farther edge. His hair was nearly all burned away. His eyes rolled white in a blackened face, and his teeth were a white slash in a gaping mouth. He yanked viciously at the quilt, attempting to tear it from Mary.

Mary did a quick turn toward him that wound her and Ida more firmly into their end of the quilt. She braced her heels in the sand of the river bottom and dug the fingers of her free hand into the most distant fold she could reach, pulling with all her might to gain it back.

The man pulled, too, using two hands and arms that were muscled like a wrestler's. He had the advantage of her in strength and in height as well. Mary made another swift turn into the quilt, but in doing so, she was forced to give ground, which brought the water level up to her chin. She leaned away from him with every ounce of leverage she could command. This quilt was her one fragile shelter from the heat, and no one was going to get it from her without a fight.

Neither she nor the man spoke. They had no breath to spare as they seesawed back and forth. Nobody around them appeared to notice the silent tug-of-war or to take an interest in its outcome, not even Mrs. Nordquist, who could not seem to stop an attack of panting and coughing.

A sudden shift of the man's position yanked Mary sideways. Her feet skidded from under her, and the tension on the quilt lurched her forward. She struck at the man's face with clawed fingers. She would have set her teeth in his arm if she had been close enough, but tangled in the quilt, weighted down by Ida, and made doubly clumsy in the water by dragging skirts and petticoats, she missed on both counts.

The man seized his chance to give the quilt another violent tug, but his efforts were driving him backward into deeper water, too. A giant log loomed up from nowhere, bearing down on them like a railway car. The man saw it before Mary did. He let go of the quilt and attempted to dive aside. Whether he was successful or whether the log struck and rolled him under, Mary was never sure. She had a glimpse of a slowly revolving P enclosed in a diamond—the brand mark the Peshtigo Company stamped into the end of each of its logs. Then she was hit a glancing blow that bowled her over but that also shoved her from the monster's path.

A flurry of desperate kicks and flailings brought her upright and onto her feet once more. The man was gone, whether drowned or merely defeated she could not tell, nor was she curious. If there had been two quilts, she would have let him have one. Or had he asked only for a share of the one she did have, she and Mrs. Nordquist would have done what they could to make room for him. But possession of that quilt might mean the difference between survival and death, and Mary found that she was not as ready to die as she had thought. On the contrary, spitting water, gasping in the heat that served for air, cradling Ida more securely against her, hauling the quilt up over them, she knew she wanted very much to live and that she was not going to give up so long as a single vital spark continued to flicker within her.

Mrs. Nordquist was at her elbow, helping with the quilt. "That log," she panted apologetically. "I did not see it coming."

"Nor I," Mary said. She considered telling her of the man, for Mrs. Nordquist apparently had not seen him either, but he was already part of the past, and breath was too precious to squander on pointless talk.

Neither was there time to spare for it. "Look there," she said instead. Then: "Watch out!"

A horse was swimming toward them. Behind it was a cow. Mary and Mrs. Nordquist started to shuffle out of the way at the best speed they could manage, but the horse's hoofs struck bottom before it was quite to the crowd of people standing in the river. Snorting and blowing, it turned and launched itself into the deeper water again, the cow following. Other cattle and horses were swimming here and there, not this close to where Mary and Mrs. Nordquist stood, but not so far off that it was safe not to keep an eye alert for them.

The logs, though, were a greater hazard. Stirred by the explosion, carried in one direction by the current, driven by the wind in another, they came drifting, bumping, jostling on erratic courses that had to be watched to be avoided. They were too huge to be maneuvered easily by a shove of an arm or several arms. Each log contained lumber enough for an entire house, Ellery had once told Mary. She was aware of a spreading pain in her shoulder from the comparatively gentle nudge she had received. And now she saw that flames were springing up on many of the logs as they moved along, bringing the fire to the center of the river.

"Give me," Mrs. Nordquist said, reaching her hands toward Ida. "I'll hold her for a while, and you can rest your arms."

This time Mary was thankful to accept the offer. That brief tug-of-war over the quilt had called a spurt of strength from her she hadn't known she owned, but the aftermath was a surge of tremors through her arms and legs that she could not seem to control. Ida, although on the small side for a two-year-old, was becoming heavier by the minute.

Ida whimpered somewhat about being transfered to Mrs. Nordquist, but she stirred only feebly a little later when Mary took her again. She was no longer kicking or squirming in protest when they had to duck under water. Perhaps she was getting used to it, Mary thought. That was better than fearing that water and smoke and heat and terror could break her hold on life without the flames ever touching her. Even if the fear were true, there was nothing different Mary could do, no other way to help.

She and Mrs. Nordquist went on taking turns holding Ida and splashing water on each other as glowing coals and hot ashes sifted down on them.

Mary was not certain just when she noticed that the light was changing. She thought at first it was a trick of the smoke or else that her eyes were failing her. The light was dimming somewhat, the glare less fierce. She lowered her eyes to a charred barrel stave bobbing on the water near her, then looked toward the shore again.

It was true. A margin of darkness, of night sky, showed above the flames on the west shore. The flames were slowly, very slowly but most surely, sinking.

Little by little, the margin of darkness widened and spread. The flames on the east shore were growing lower, too. A strange sort of twilight settled over the river. The heat became gradually less intense.

Mary realized that the intervals she and Mrs. Nordquist could stand to be above the water without submerging themselves were getting longer. By the end of perhaps another hour, they didn't have to submerge at all. It was enough simply to splash water on themselves from time to time. People began leaving the deeper water and venturing closer to the shore, pausing where the water reached only to their waists or to their thighs. Cautiously Mary and Mrs. Nordquist moved into the shallows, too.

Darkness never did wholly cover the river that night. By the time the last of the flames died out, dawn was paling the sky. Even then a patch of embers glowed here and an isolated tongue of flame flickered there.

Mary had seen other dawns, but never had she experienced one like this. She wanted never to repeat it.

A terrible stillness lay on the earth after the uproar and activity of the night. No rooster crowed. No bird chirped. No leaf fluttered in the breeze. No leaf nor bird nor rooster remained in the flat, black desolation that had been a town and a forest. The very wind itself was gone. Dead. Only the smoke continued to hang low and thick.

But stillness was not the same as silence. All up and down the river there were sobbings and whimperings and moanings, the sounds of people in pain. Two or three hardy souls waded to the bank to test the ground, but they did not climb out onto it. Word passed through the crowds in the water that the earth was too hot to bear underfoot.

Mary knelt in the shallows and sat hunched on her heels to wait. She had been standing all through the night, and without warning, her legs did not want to hold her any more. Her teeth were chattering and she was shivering from head to foot, for the river was colder than ever without the fire heat to offset it. Her sodden garments were pasted to her in chill layers.

Ida's little frame was shaking, too. Mary started to rub her hand up and down the child's leg to warm it. Her hand was instantly raked by such pain that she cried out. She stared at the crisscross of oozing blisters she had just broken open.

As if that discovery were a signal, a blaze of heat awoke in the back of her hand, her other hand, her wrists, her arms, her shoulders, her face, her ears, and places where she did not think she could have possibly been burned. It was as if all her flesh were on fire from the inside. She plunged her arm into the cold water clear to the shoulder, then patted soothing water on her face and ears, but the relief that brought was only temporary. In a moment the burning was hotter than before. She could not help sobbing aloud from the pain, but it didn't matter, for so many others were doing the same. And yet, with her skin on fire, she went on shivering from the cold.

She was so overwhelmed by her own misery for a while that she almost forgot about Mrs. Nordquist. When at last she turned her head to look at her, it was because Mrs. Nordquist had rested her fingers on Mary's arm. Mary flinched without meaning to. It hurt to be touched even lightly. But the older woman's eyes, staring at her through eyelids puffed nearly shut, had an earnestness that held Mary's attention.

"You tell him—" The voice was a croak from a raw and parched throat. "—when he come—Sigvard, you tell him—" She paused for breath, and the next words were a jumble of sound that Mary could not make out.

"What?" she said, and her own voice was a worse croak than Mrs. Nordquist's.

"Sigvard— Tell him—" The hand pressed harder on Mary's arm as Mrs. Nordquist swayed where she knelt. She coughed and laboriously steadied herself, but her words again became a jumble of Norwegian and English that Mary could barely hear, much less understand. "Good boy—all gone . . ."

Suddenly Mary did understand, not the words but what they meant. Mrs. Nordquist was leaving Sigvard a message because she did not expect to be able to tell him herself when—or if—he found them. Mrs. Nordquist had been sick and in need of medication before the fire; she was a great deal sicker now.

"No!" Mary interrupted her in a panic. "You'll be all right. You'll be fine."

A man was walking on the riverbank. He was moving carefully, but it was plain that the heat of the sand had cooled enough so that he was not being driven back to the water.

Warm sand, warm and dry, a place to lie down. The thought of it brought Mary to her feet. She cupped her hand under Mrs. Nordquist's elbow, in spite of the hurt, and pulled her to her feet. "Come on."

It was a peculiar sensation, stumbling up onto dry land after so many hours of being buoyed and pushed by the water. The weight of her legs came as a surprise. Mrs. Nordquist leaned on her more heavily at each step and began to pant as if the burden were hers.

A few feet from the water's edge, Mary set Ida down, hoping to coax her to walk alongside her. Ida curled down immediately into the heated sand, and wouldn't even try to stand. Mary was too weary herself to drag her or Sigvard's aunt or the leaden quilt any farther. She sank down beside Ida, and Mrs. Nordquist dropped in a wheezing heap next to her.

They just lay there, the three of them, welcoming the warmth of the ground that was almost too hot for comfort and yet not hot enough to conquer their shiverings. Mary sat up once to spread the damp quilt over them. It was drying quickly in the open air, and she thought it might help concentrate the warmth around them. Also, its cool dampness was a little soothing to her burns, which felt like live coals. Ida whimpered a protest and squirmed to push the quilt away, but Mrs. Nordquist accepted her portion of it with a deep sigh and a murmur. She did not stir.

Mrs. Nordquist would be all right, Mary told herself. At least, she would be as all right as anyone could be after the ordeal they had been through. Mary's concern for her eased a little. The dreadful night they had just shared was like a bond of kinship. They had to stay responsible for each other, because who else was there now who cared?

Ellery, went through her mind. Where was he? What had happened to him? And Clara? The other children? But she didn't want to think about them quite yet. She was afraid to think about what might be.

Someone was running along the riverbank and calling questions to people as they straggled out of the water. "Is the priest there? Father Pernin? There's a woman needs the priest—"

Did that mean the woman was dying? Mary wondered. She lay listening to the man repeating his question farther on and to the voices that answered him here and there. To have lived through the fire, only to die afterward—somehow that was worse than death at the height of the fire. The unfairness of it made her angry.

She sat up as if it were important to demonstrate that Mary James was still very much alive and determined to remain so.

A small hand grabbed at her skirt, and Ida was staring up at her out of red-rimmed, sore-looking eyes. "Ma'y!"

"It's all right. I'm not leaving you."

Mary drew her closer and began to examine her inch by inch for signs of damage. Several locks of blonde baby hair were singed and darkened, and the back of one hand bore a huge, puffy blister that nearly covered it, but other than that, Ida appeared unscathed. Her clothes and the woolen shawl wrapped around her, plus the protection of the quilt, had gone far to save her. Even her shoes, which Mary had thrust onto her feet without lingering to button them, were intact aside from being somewhat waterlogged.

"Wan' go home," Ida said. She pulled at Mary's skirt and a fragment came away in her hand. The petticoat beneath was scorched brittle, too. "Ma'y," Ida repeated, unimpressed, "wan' go home."

"We can't go home. It isn't there. It's all burned up," Mary said, but she heard her words as if they were being spoken by someone else, someone who was telling her something she knew was true but which she could not really believe.

Gone. All burned up. Nothing left. The clock above the stove, the horsehair chair in the parlor, the furnishings of the little room she had slept in, the room itself, the fences, the shed, the chickens in the yard, her green dress and her trunk—everything gone.

"No!" Ida scrambled to her feet. "Go home! Go home!"

She started to cry. The sobs quickly became a coughing fit that sat her down on the quilt, then tumbled her over onto her knees and hands. Her breath caught somewhere, and she wilted, gasping, turning blue, onto the quilt.

Mary picked her up and patted her on the back, pounded her, shook her. At last, short, ragged breaths began to wheeze from Ida's open mouth and her lips slowly took on a faint pink tone, but her store of energy was gone. She lay quietly on the quilt, curled on her side, too spent to cry again.

Mary forgot some of her own hurting in watching the shallow in-and-out rhythm of her breathing. Why couldn't there be a breeze to lift and thin the smoke from the air? That was what was doing the damage, the smoke that hung on as if it were a torment quite separate from the fire. The fire had a beginning and an end, but the smoke—would they ever be free of it?

She sniffed the air. Her stomach did a sickening turn as she recognized the odor that had come into the smoke during the night. It was an odor she had smelled only once before. She had smelled it the summer she was twelve, when lightning had struck a neighbor's barn down the road. A pig, a cow, a team of horses and a half dozen sheep had been lost in the fire, and the odor of flesh charred to cinders had hung over the site for days.

"Mary? Mary?" A man was questing along the bank, coming toward her.

Mary lurched to her feet, stepping on her skirt in her haste and tearing away another portion of the weakened material. "Here! Over here!"

He broke into a limping run, and she saw that one pants leg hung in burned tatters up to above his knee and that the boot he wore on that foot was a broken mass of brittle, curling leather. Half his beard was burned away and the other half badly singed, giving his smoke-blackened features a lopsided effect that made it hard to tell at first glance if he were friend or stranger. She let herself believe for the fraction of a second that he could be Ellery—but he was not.

"Have you seen her?" he asked, peering eagerly into Mary's face. "My wife? Mary, Mary Jenkins. A little taller than you, dark hair, blue eyes. We got separated on the bridge. Have you seen her?"

Mary concentrated on recalling the faces that had been near her in the river. She was surprised that they were mainly a blur. Her attention had been on the fire and on the other menaces of logs and swimming livestock, rather than on her fellow refugees.

She shook her head slowly, hating to disappoint the man's hopes. What disappointments were in store for her in her turn?

"I'm sorry. My name's Mary, too. I thought maybe you

were my brother-in-law. Have you seen him? Ellery Cody?"

"Cody? I know him, but no, I haven't seen him." The man paused, as if thinking. "Not him, but—"

He paused again, looked hard at her and looked away. "No, I didn't see him, but I'll pass the word along."

Mary stepped in front of him to keep him from limping off. "But what? You said, 'Not him, but—' What did you see? Tell me. Please."

"I'm not sure. It might not have been the same—Anyway, it doesn't have to mean anything." He glanced down at his burned leg, then up at her and made up his mind. "Over on Oconto Avenue, I saw that mustang he's been driving. At least, I thought it was his horse. And his wagon. They cut through the Catholic church property, going like fury, and the wagon went over. But there was nobody in it. I swear there was nobody in it."

Mary's throat closed on itself. She could not ask why Ellery had not been in his wagon nor what had become of him. If he had fallen from it— If the horse had bolted and left him behind—

Her knees went spongy, and she sank down on the quilt beside Ida while the man, Mr. Jenkins, moved on. She heard him repeat his questions about his wife to a man and woman a few yards away, and saw them shake their heads.

Behind Mary somewhere a woman was sobbing. Mary did not want to look, but her head was drawn around toward the sound in spite of herself. The woman, clad in blackened tatters of what must last night have been a nightgown, was kneeling by the body of a man lying on the sand a short distance from the river. He had been there, lying face down, when Mary climbed out of the water, and she had supposed without really thinking about it that he must be one of the first to find the hot sand bearable. Now she realized that, although his body appeared not to have been touched by flames, he was one who had never reached the river. He was dead.

Mary bent her face over Ida. She gathered the little girl into her lap, needing the reassurance of something warm and alive in her arms. If no one came for them soon, she, too, would be obliged to set out in search of her family. And if she found them among the dead, what would she do?

"Sigvard?" Mrs. Nordquist was struggling to sit up.

"No," Mary said, following the line of the older woman's gaze. "His name is Jenkins. He was looking for his wife."

"Sigvard," Mrs. Nordquist repeated as if she did not understand. Then: "Is there water?"

"I'll get some."

Mary slipped Ida to the quilt and got unsteadily to her feet. The soles of her feet were blistered, and it hurt to walk. Her shoes were no help, for when she pulled one off at the edge of the water, thinking it might serve as a dipper, she found that the sole was burned through. The sole of the other shoe had burned through in two places.

A gray film of ash lay on the water's surface. She dipped beneath it to the depth of her elbows, scooped up as much as her cupped hands would hold and hobbled back to the quilt.

Through her mind flitted the image of Sigvard as she had seen him last, running into the flames to try to rescue a lost child, and she knew why she had not asked Mr. Jenkins for word of him as well. She did not have even a hope that Sigvard had survived.

Mrs. Nordquist barely moistened her lips with the water before she sank down on the sand again. Beneath its dark smudges of smoke and soot, her skin was a pallid gray. Her eyes, not dark like Sigvard's but a clear, light blue, widened into a stare fixed on something above and beyond Mary's left shoulder. Mary glanced around, but there was nothing to see in that direction—nothing but the ash-dulled flatness of the river and the blackened flatness of the other side.

"Mrs. Nordquist," she urged. "Can't I help you? Are you sick? What should I do?"

For answer, there was only the breath that passed in and out through Mrs. Nordquist's parted lips.

Mary half-rose to her feet once more, meaning to run for help. But where to go? Who to ask? Not Mr. Jenkins, now a tiny figure far up the river, stopping to question still another group of people. Not the woman mourning the dead man nearby, for two young boys were with her now, themselves sobbing while they tried without much success to draw her away. Not the cluster of people huddled together a scant foot or two from the water—half a dozen children of various ages, all of them crying, a woman who lay in the warm ashes as if she would never stir again, and a man who sat hunched so close to the water that his feet remained in it. What help could anyone give, anyway, when nowhere any more was there a bed to lie in, a shelter to be carried to, or so much as a spoon or a cup in which to measure out medicine, much less any medicine to be measured?

Ida rolled onto her hands and knees and tugged at Mary's ankle. "Going home?" she asked hopefully.

Mary felt a rush of tears crowding her throat and welling over her lashes. She fought against them because of the sting they brought to her already sore and swollen eyes. And because, if once she let go, she feared she might shatter into too many pieces ever to be put back together again.

A solitary man was wandering along the river, peering into faces, pausing here and there to ask a question, as were a number of other men and women now. "Please!" Mary called to him when he looked her way. "Will you help us? Please!"

He nodded and quickened his pace, but his stride was uneven as if the soles of his feet, too, were tender. His coat was gone, and his shirt was hardly more than a scorched remnant stuffed into the top of trousers that were not much better. He was a big man, broad through the shoulders and tall, and he walked with a military erectness that was suddenly as familiar to Mary as her own heartbeat.

She pressed a hand to her mouth, not daring to believe the truth of what she felt rather than saw as he drew near. His hair might have been any color under its streaks of soot, and the smoke-grimed face was fringed by only a scorched and ragged stubble of what once had been a silken beard. The eyebrows were singed away entirely. And yet his eyes, those blue, blue eyes—surely she could not be mistaken about them.

"Ellery?"

He halted. Grooves of concentration wrinkled the odd blankness of his forehead as he stared at her. A whisper of alarm like a voice from another world chilled her for an instant: have I changed that much, too?

"Mary!" He started forward. "Mary, is it you?"

She flung herself into his arms, and he hugged her close, both of them laughing and crying. Mary buried her face against his shoulder, heedless of the protest that blazed up in her burned hands and arms as she clung to him. Nothing was important for the moment except that he was alive and he was here, and that at last she was safe. Her fears, her uncertainties, the burden of responsibilities—she could lay them all aside now and trust in him.

He hugged her once more and released her. "Where's Clara?"

Her elation lost a share of its glow. "I—I don't know. She and Tat and Nettie were ahead of me, and I got too far behind, somehow. But they were ahead of me on French Street." If Ellery were safe, she could not believe that real harm could have come to any of the others. "They would have reached the bridge before I did. They must have got across in plenty of time."

She stooped to the baby and lifted her. "Here's Ida. She's pretty much as good as new."

"Ida." Ellery picked her up and smoothed her rumpled hair. The little girl submitted uneasily, frowning into his face as if not quite decided who he was.

"And who's that?" Ellery asked, nodding toward Mrs. Nordquist.

"Oh, my gracious! Sigvard's aunt!" Mary dropped to her knees beside her in a wash of guilt. She had almost forgotten about Mrs. Nordquist. "Sigvard got us here to the river, but we haven't seen him since, and she's sick. She needs him, and I don't know what to do."

"There's nothing you can do. If Sig knows where to look for her, he'll find her." Ellery reached for Mary's elbow to help raise her to her feet. "Let's go. Maybe Clara got down as far as the dam."

Mary resisted the pressure on her elbow. "You mean just leave her here? What if Sig doesn't come? Who's left to help her?"

"There are plenty of people around. No harm's going to come to her here." Impatience roughened Ellery's voice. "You have to set priorities like on a battlefield. The unfit, the wounded, they have to wait their turn."

Still Mary hesitated. It went against the grain to desert the woman like this. And didn't she owe it to her and Sigvard to stay by her?

She smoothed the quilt more fully over Mrs. Nordquist's shoulders. At least that frightening spasm or seizure or whatever it was had passed. The poor woman was lying quietly now, her eyes almost closed and the harsh note of her breathing no longer audible.

Mary tilted her head, listening with abrupt intentness. Her hand sought under the quilt for Mrs. Nordquist's wrist. There was no faintest flutter of a pulse.

Very gently and with a calm that surprised her, she pulled the corner of the quilt up over the work-lined face and stood up. "All right. We can go. She's dead."

Ellery slipped her arm through his without a word. He took two or three steps, then stopped and turned back. "We'll be needing this more than her," he said, and piled the quilt into Mary's arms.

He was right, of course. Concern for the living had to come ahead of consideration for the dead. But the bulky armload kept her from taking his arm again. Without altogether understanding why, she limped a fraction more slowly as they moved on down the river until she was walking behind Ellery, not at his side.

THAT WALK ALONG the river in search of Clara was the longest of Mary's life. She had thought if she could only survive the flames and those endless hours of chill water and searing smoke she would have lived through the nightmare and would be able to put it behind her. Limping on throbbing feet from one dismal cluster of people to another, peering anxiously into every blackened face, asking and answering the same questions over and over with always the same disheartening responses, she knew that the nightmare was only just beginning.

A woman holding a tiny baby put out a hand to touch Ida. "Yours?" she asked Ellery.

"Mine," he said.

"You haven't seen one that size—a boy? He was wearing a flannel shirt and checked apron. I had his hand almost to the river . . ."

Ellery shook his head. "I'm sorry. But maybe you've seen my wife. Big-boned woman, dark red hair, in the family way?"

"She has two children with her, a boy of four and a five-year-old girl," Mary added.

It was the woman's turn to shake her head. "They say a woman gave birth last night in the water. But they said it was her first." She gestured vaguely downstream, then cradled her own baby closer. "They're dead, the baby and the mother. But my little boy's two—flannel shirt and checked apron—"

She moved on, and Mary no longer had to look at the baby, who lay limp as a doll in its mother's arms. It, too, was dead.

She wanted to tell Ellery, "That isn't Clara, the woman she heard of. It couldn't be Clara."

She did not tell him because he was already striding on ahead of her; and also because a foreboding was beginning to choke her like the smoke-laden air. They would not find Clara alive if they found her at all. That was the price that would be exacted from Mary for coveting Ellery and wishing Clara out of the way.

Three woman lay huddled beneath a grimy, ash-streaked blanket. The one in the middle rolled her head to and fro on the sand. She was croaking, "Help! We're on fire! Help us."

Ellery stooped for a closer view of her, then of her companions. "You're not on fire," he said, straightening. "The fire's gone."

"We're burning," the woman insisted. "Please, help us. We're burning up!"

Neither of her companions stirred. The nearer one might

have been asleep, but a sharper glance told Mary that that was not true of either of them. They had not been burned, at least nowhere that was visible. But the evidences of death were becoming ever more familiar to Mary.

And I don't feel anything about it, she thought with a faint wonder that was not the same as surprise. All I care is that none of them is Clara.

"Help us!" The woman in the middle twisted under the blanket. "We're on fire! We're burning up! Someone help us. Please!"

Mary was about to limp on after Ellery, but the terror in the woman's cry held her. She knew this woman from church, although she could not fit a name to her.

"No, you're not on fire. The fire's gone. You're not going to burn up."

The woman gazed up at her from wild, smoke-reddened eyes. "Please! We're burning. Pour water on us, somebody, please! Put the fire out."

Mary stared around her helplessly. The river was only a few yards from where she stood, but there was nothing anywhere that could serve to carry water, nothing anywhere but barren, blackened earth and ashes.

A man paused beside her and cocked his head toward the moaning woman's pleas. Without a word, he trudged on down the riverbank to the water and brought back his brimless remnant of a hat full of water.

"It's all right, Mrs. Whitney." He sloshed the contents of the hat over the woman's head and the upper edge of the blanket. "It's all right."

The hat contained hardly a dipperful of water, but the

woman's twisting and crying stopped. She relaxed and lay quiet, while trickles of water smeared the ash streaks on her cheeks and soaked into the singed ends of her hair.

The man jammed the wet hat back onto his head. He crowded his hands into the pockets of trousers that were charred tatters halfway to the knee, and shook his head slowly at the three figures covered by the blanket.

Mary was anxious to follow Ellery, who with Ida drooping against his shoulder, was getting steadily farther away, never doubting, apparently, that Mary was right at his heels. Something about the man in the hat, however, prompted her to take a second look. His face was seamed by a broad welt of a burn just above where the eyebrows used to be.

"Mr. Collins?"

"Yes." He blinked at her and peered through puffed red eyelids. "And you're—"

Again that feather of dread that had brushed her when Ellery found it difficult to recognize her. Did tumbled hair and a coating of soot make all that much difference? "Mary James," she said. "Clara Cody's sister."

"Mary. Yes." Now there was recognition, but with it a rueful—surely not pitying—shake of his head that was more disconcerting than not being recognized. He achieved a small smile. "Well, you're safe. You made it through, thank God. You haven't come across Jewel this morning, have you? Some fellow told me he thought he'd seen her above the bridge, in the river."

Mary's disquiet about herself vanished in a shiver that was more than just the river chill that still clung to her. She shook her head slowly, bundling the unwieldy quilt tighter in her arms as though its gritty folds could ward off the need to speak the truth.

"You haven't seen her?" Mr. Collins prompted. "Nor heard anything of her? She was spending the night up the street at her friend, Minnie's . . ." His voice trailed off as Mary continued to shake her head. "You don't know?"

"No, I saw her." Mary swallowed against a swelling wedge in her throat. "She's not—She didn't—"

The words would not come. Only the realization that she was not as numb to every feeling as she had thought. She stared at the once jolly little man, willing him to grasp her message without forcing her to go on.

"Tell me," he commanded.

"Mr. Collins, she—Jewel—didn't get to the river. She was running, but there was a shower of sparks and she—she went down."

"You saw her? Jewel? You're certain?"

Mary nodded. The temptation was strong to say she was not absolutely certain, that it was possible that in all the turmoil she had mistaken another girl for Jewel, but something warned her that in the end the lie would be a greater cruelty than the truth.

"Where?" Mr. Collins asked.

"On French Street. About half a block from the bridge."

She groped in her mind for something more to say. Ma would have known the right thing to say; perhaps even Clara in her blunt way, but Mary could find nothing but an inadequate, "I'm sorry."

"Yes," Mr. Collins said vaguely as if he had not really heard her anyway. "I'll have to tell her mother."

But he made no move that would indicate where Mrs. Collins might be. Instead, he lifted off his wet hat and stood revolving it carefully in his hands as if he might locate its missing brim by examining it closely enough.

"Mary!" Ellery was retracing his steps. "What are you doing? I thought you were going to stick close to me. Who's this? Collins?"

"Cody?" Mr. Collins accepted the hand Ellery extended to him and let his arm be pumped.

"Glad to see you made it through," Ellery told him. "It was touch and go with me for a while. I was out west of town, and the blasted horse bolted with the wagon. Left me to leg it, and no chance to get back to my family. I'm still hunting for them."

"Yes, we made it," Mr. Collins said to his mangled hat. "My wife and me, we made it. But not our girl. We lost our girl."

Ellery muttered a sound in his throat and dropped his hand onto Mr. Collins's shoulder. "I never saw the beat of this, not in all the years of the war. It always seemed there was some sense to things in the war."

Mr. Collins gave himself a small shake, like a man trying to wake up. "Ellen's down the river a way. She's doing what she can to help some of the others. I think your wife's down there, too."

Mary was startled by the oath that burst from Ellery, but she could hardly blame him. "You mean you know where she is, my wife? She's all right? Why didn't you tell me?"

She did feel a twinge of compassion for Mr. Collins beneath the relief that flooded her. It wasn't quite fair to expect his first thought to have been of their anxieties and of Clara, under the circumstances. Still, it was not easy to be patient while he slowly replaced his hat on his head and turned to lead the way.

Half a dozen strides put Ellery in the lead as soon as he understood where they were heading. Mary could only marvel at his stamina. He must be as worn as anyone else by the long night of fire and water and watching, but he carried Ida as lightly and swung along as firmly as if the ordeal that would drain an ordinary man had barely touched him.

Her admiration was gradually tempered, however, by the strain of trying to keep up with the pace he set. She had been too absorbed in fear and self-accusation before to give thought to how painful it was to hobble on her blistered feet in their broken shoes. The blisters were open sores now, their steady smarting jolting into fresh jabs of fire at each step. She was aware, too, of a heavy throbbing in her left shoulder which had been going on for a long time. Was that where the log had struck her in the water when she was fighting to hang onto the quilt? The quilt itself was beginning to drag at her arms as if it were weighted with rocks.

A hand eased itself beneath her elbow. She leaned into its support gratefully. It was odd that Mr. Collins should put her in mind of Pa when the two of them were nothing alike in age or appearance.

But she put the thought of Pa from her quickly before needing him, his confidence and strength, grew into a longing too great for her to bear. Ellery would take care of them. If anybody could get them through all this, it would be him.

"Not very much farther now," Mr. Collins said. "I doubt

your sister has moved on to look for you. I doubt she'd try. But you can't be sure."

Who could be sure of what Clara might do next, Mary reflected—but with a flicker of pride that surprised her. They wouldn't find Clara in a state of hysteria like the woman back there convinced her blanket was still burning. Nor would Clara be dazed out of her senses like that younger woman cuddling a baby she did not appear to know was dead. Clara wouldn't be swallowed in self-pity like the man they were passing now, who sat with his head resting on his drawn-up knees, ignoring the woman and two half-grown youngsters crouched beside him while he moaned over and over, "God! Oh, God! Oh, God!"

"We'll find her, whatever," Mary said. "Just so long as she's—"

But she bit down on the final word, turning it into a cough before it was spoken. Not even she could be so thoughtless as to rejoice aloud in Clara's being alive to a man whose own quest for those who belonged to him had ended on such a different note.

She averted her eyes from Mr. Collins and was gazing down at the carcass of a horse, its head and neck stretched toward the water it had never reached. The fire's heat had shrunk the body to two-thirds of its natural size, reducing it to a grotesque caricature of a horse. Ellery stepped over the blackened mound without a second glance, but neither Mary's legs nor her nerves were equal to that. She buried her nose in a fold of the quilt as Mr. Collins steered her around the creature. Her stomach doubled on itself convulsively all the same at the heavy burn stench that hung in the air above the carcass. She heard Mr. Collins make a small, strangling noise in his throat.

A dozen yards farther on a child was weeping hopelessly within the shelter of a dilapidated quilt. The woman who shared the quilt was patting and rocking her in an attempt to soothe, but the woman herself drooped as if she were too sick to put much force into the effort. Her face was hidden by the ruin of a bonnet, and she did not look up as Ellery tramped past her.

Mary very nearly passed her by, too. There were so many such scenes—crying children, exhausted parents—scattered in every direction, and so little anyone could do to help. Besides, her mind was on locating a woman who would have two small children with her: Tat and Netty.

Mr. Collins began to say something, just as the weeping child interrupted herself with a shriek: "Ida!"

Ida's head bobbed up from its resting place on Ellery's shoulder. The older child flung off the quilt and scrambled up in a staggering run. "Ida! Papa!"

Tear streaks and smudges through the grime on the square little face gave it the startling appearance of a savage's painted for battle, but the ragged pigtails that stood out behind her ears and blazed as bright as scrubbed carrots were unmistakable even in the smoke haze.

"Netty!" Mary sprang forward, forgetful of her burned feet and Mr. Collins's steadying hand. "Ellery, it's Netty. And—" the shape of the woman still seated on the ground and half-sheathed in the quilt took on sudden, sure identity—"Clara! They're here, Ellery. Here they are!"

Ellery was turning, setting Ida on her feet, bending to

loosen Netty's locked arms from around his knees, laughing, clucking to the children as if they were horses.

"Mary, is that you?" Clara called. "Ellery? Where are you? I can't see."

She pushed up the wilted brim of her bonnet. Beneath it, her face was one angry swelling. Only a crease in the puffed red flesh marked where eyes should have been.

Mary dropped onto her knees beside Clara."We're here. Ellery's safe, and he found us all, so you don't have to worry. But what's happened to you? Are you burned? Where?"

"Burned some, yes," Clara said. "But not so much as others. It's the smoke, I think. Made me sick. And my hip. It gave out on me just as we were getting up on the bank, I couldn't get any farther."

Mary was alarmed as much by the thinness of the voice as by the reasons for it. She had heard Clara when she sounded tired and when she was headachy and when she had claimed that her nerves were on edge, but never, never before had it been a sound so utterly drained of vitality as this.

Mary sent a frightened glance up at Ellery as he slid his arm around Clara's shoulders and folded his length down next to her. "There now, don't you fret, Mother. Just lean back and relax until you get your bearings, and you'll be fine. There's no place you have to get to right now; no place left to get to, anyway."

Clara did relax against him, or rather, she settled into the angle of his shoulder and arm like a bundle of rags that had no inner bracing of its own. She put a red and blistered hand to her eyes, then let it fall away. "I can't see— Everything's gone, is it?"

"Pretty near everything. Some holes in the ground that used to be cellars, and I guess the bridge pilings down at the waterline, logs from the mill pond and the dam. Not much else. Except the most important thing: us. That's what counts after a battle—whether you made it through alive or not, and we did."

Listening to him, Mary almost believed there was nothing more that did matter. But she was reminded, too, of Mr. Collins and his loss. She looked around for him in vain. Quietly and without waiting for thanks, he had drifted away to complete his personal errand of finding Mrs. Collins and telling her what must be told.

"Poor Netty," Clara began. "Her knees—" A spasm of coughing stopped her.

"I fell down where the sidewalk was on fire," Netty explained, her voice not altogether free of sobs yet. "It burned right through my dress and petticoat. Mama tore them off."

She tugged at the wrinkled cotton stockings that for all practical purposes were the only pretense of garments she possessed from the waist down. A dollar-sized hole charred about the edges gaped below the knee of each. Fresh tears brimmed onto her cheeks, and she sat down quickly. "It hurts. It hurts."

"It doesn't hurt that bad," Ellery said as if he could persuade her this was true. "Not so a big girl like you wants to cry. Look at Ida here. She's got a blister the size of your thumb on her hand, and she's not crying."

Ida regarded the white welt at the base of her fingers, pleased by her father's evident interest in it. "Big worm," she croaked in her smoke-roughened voice.

But blisters not yet rubbed open did not hurt, Mary reflected. Neither did burns like the round, whitish one on the inside of her wrist, which she had acquired she did not know where. But there were other sorts, redder ones, that she could testify continued to burn as if fire were trapped in them. It was asking a great deal of a child of five to hold back the tears that even a young woman of seventeen had to keep winking to control.

"Maybe if we pull your stockings around so where they're still wet can cover the hurt," she suggested without much faith in the remedy. "Anyway, let's try."

Netty scuttled closer to her and thrust her feet into Mary's lap with a gasp and a shudder that left no doubt as to how real the pain was.

Clara's head moved against Ellery's shoulder. "Where's Tat?"

"I don't know. I haven't seen him." Ellery shifted slightly to scan the area around them. "It's like him to wander off."

A terrible premonition chilled the nape of Mary's neck. Her fingers, fumbling to smooth Netty's stocking, went stiff. She knew before Clara spoke it, what the answer was going to be:

"Tat was with Mary."

"He was with you. I saw him. He wouldn't stay with me. He twisted loose and ran ahead, and I couldn't get hold of him again. But he caught up to you and Netty. I saw him. I'm sure I did."

Mary heard the rising tremor in the words and stopped. She was trembling all over, she realized. She had to struggle for a dizzy moment to keep from being sick.

"I thought he was with you," Clara repeated. It was not an accusation nor a reproach. It was more like a request for Mary—for anyone—to undo the fact that could not be undone.

"Where was it that you lost him?" Ellery asked. "Where were you?"

"Around the corner from the house. We were running toward French Street. The wind knocked us down, and he was in the street. I pulled him up, and we started after Clara, but I couldn't hold him. I couldn't hold him."

But no apologies, excuses, or explanations would undo the fact, either. Tat had somehow been left behind. "I was so sure I saw him catch up to Clara," Mary finished in a whisper directed at no one. "All this time I was so sure he must be with her."

Ellery sat and looked at her, saying nothing. Muscles worked along his singed jaw and at the edges of his mouth, too visible now that his beard was gone. Then he bent his head into his hand, covering his eyes, and released a sigh that was very close to a groan and that said everything.

In spite of her efforts to shut out the memory, Mary was gazing again at the unknown little boy whose body she had stumbled over in the street. She could not remember his face. In her mind's eye now, it was Tat's.

CLARA MADE A CHOKING sound and began to cough until she was gasping for breath. When she could speak, she whispered, "Let me lie down."

Mary leaned to catch her as she slumped away from Ellery's support, but Ellery tightened his arm and lowered her gently if somewhat awkwardly to the ground. Together he and Mary straightened the quilt under her as best they could, while Netty, whimpering, worked to drag her own stockings around to cool her burns.

"What?"Mary asked as Clara's swollen lips framed a weak murmur.

"Cold," Clara said. "So chilly."

She was shivering, although the heat radiating from her skin was strong enough for Mary to feel on her face as she stooped close.

"Here—" said Mary. "This other quilt."

She stood up and shook out the quilt she had carried so far. She spread it over Clara, taking exquisite care to mound it around her shoulders and tuck it over her feet. There was little enough she could do to make amends to Clara for the terrible things she had done already. Even the fresh throbbings the actions woke in her shoulder and raw hands she welcomed as a just part of her penance.

And Ellery had been right: they did need the extra quilt more than Mrs. Nordquist could. Mary cast a glance at him, wanting to apologize, she was not sure why. She had never really doubted he was right.

Ellery took no notice of her. He sat with bowed shoulders, one hand resting on the quilt where it covered Clara's arm. Ida was nestling herself under his other arm, but he was not noticing her, either. He was staring across the river into the hazy emptiness where the town had stood.

Netty had given up fussing with her uncooperative stockings. She was a small huddle of misery at her mother's feet, alternately cupping her hands over her burned knees and jerking them away when they came too close to the hurt. Tears continued to trickle down her face, but her gulps and snuffles had a quieter, almost resigned quality to them.

Mary knelt again and drew the bent head against her good shoulder. "Burns that hurt worst heal fastest. In another day or two, you'll be mended good as new."

Mary wondered at her own glibness. Was this bit of comfort a spur-of-the-moment invention on her part, or was it something she had heard Ma say once long ago? Ma and Pa and that faraway world of peace and security and contentment—it was like trying to remember details from a fading dream.

Netty rubbed a fist across her eyes. "Did Tat get burned up?"

"We don't know." Mary gathered in a slow, level breath. "Maybe he got to the river by himself. Maybe somebody found him and took him along. Maybe we'll find him waiting for us, safe and sound, some place."

"He wouldn't hold my hand," Netty said. "Mama said hold hands, but he wouldn't. He'd only take Papa's hand."

"Hush." Mary patted her and sought for a new topic. She wasn't equal to hearing a prolonged discussion of Tat, and she supposed Ellery and Clara might not be, either. "What became of your shoes, Netty? You don't have any shoes."

"They came off in the river. They got lost in the water." Netty curved her hands toward her knees, then pulled back, heaving a tearful sigh. "Did the man get burned up, too?"

"What man?" Mary's attention was distracted by a rumble within her. Her stomach was complaining that it was empty. She had forgotten there was such a thing as eating, and the reminder struck her as somewhat indecent and petty, not to mention impossible to satisfy. But it was also surprisingly sharp.

"I told you," Netty said, aggrieved. "The man that Tat went with."

"Tat went with a man?" Mary was suddenly listening. "Tell me about him. What kind of man? Why did he take Tat with him?"

"Tat ran and grabbed his hand. He said it was Papa, but I didn't go. I held onto Mama's hand like she told me, even when I fell down." Netty plucked at her stocking and added in a final burst of righteousness, "And it wasn't Papa, anyhow."

"But the man did take Tat along with him? He didn't leave him behind? You're sure?"

Netty weighed this new urgency of interest in her story and eased her thumb into her mouth. Her answer was a mute bob of the head.

"Where were you when it happened? When Tat grabbed the man," Mary pressed. "Do you remember?"

Netty's expression grew vague. "In the road, when we was running. When the fire was coming."

She shifted restlessly and reached once more for her drawn-up knees. It was a hint that each further answer Mary might pry out of her was likely to be more vague than the last.

Mary pressed the quilt where it covered Clara's shoulder. "Did you hear? Do you remember? That man, whoever he was, he'd have looked after Tat from then on, don't you suppose?"

Clara's head rolled from one side to the other. "I'm trying to think. Maybe—" she whispered. "I—can't remember."

"But it could be he's safe, that there's a chance we'll find him." Mary could not recall ever wanting so desperately to be able to believe something. "Shouldn't we at least try to find him? Ellery?"

Ellery's hand curved to tug at the ragged stubble of his beard and drew away quickly in a gesture very like Netty's efforts to caress her knees. "I talked to just about everybody I saw from about half a mile above the factory down to here. I'd have seen him if he was there."

"But you were asking for us, weren't you? For Clara and me? You weren't really looking for him, not all by himself." Mary collected her legs under her, willing to set out on the search immediately herself, but a jolt of hot pain caused her to shift her weight from her feet at once.

"I don't know—" Ellery scrubbed a hand across his eyes. He turned to scan the riverbank up and down without rising from where he sat. His attention returned to the mounded quilt beside him, and he smoothed a rumpled corner. "Mother?"

Why was he delaying? Was he that certain there was no hope? Or was he afraid the loss would be doubly keen if their hopes were disappointed?

Something of that same fear sharpened Mary's voice to an edge she would never otherwise have used toward Ellery. "I'll look after Clara. We'll be all right. We'll be here waiting when you get back."

Ellery stood up slowly, a frown between his eyes as though his mind were somewhere else.

"Papa?" Ida caught at the tatters of his trouser leg. "Eat now?" She gave her stomach an eloquent pat. "Eat?"

"Me, too, Papa." Netty stopped nursing her knees long enough to raise her head and chime in. "I'm hungry."

"Hung'y," Ida echoed on a small hiccup that could easily become a sob. "Eat."

Incredibly, the sun, or at any rate the indistinct halo of light overhead that Mary assumed to be the sun, was indicating an hour past midmorning and well beyond the time for breakfast on an ordinary day.

"Papa can't feed you. There isn't anything to eat. It's all

burned up." Ellery stooped and detached himself from Ida's fingers. "You be good girls. Mind Mary and don't cry, and maybe Papa can find something to bring back."

Ida did cry, however, and after a minute's blank stare at her father's departing figure, so did Netty. Mary had no comfort to offer them but sympathy, which she could tell from the growing hollowness inside herself, was no comfort at all. Through her mind flitted an inventory of the pantry shelves they had left behind: jars of preserves, a loaf of bread, the half-eaten ham, a crock of butter, the tin box that housed several dozen of Clara's delicious, melt-in-the-mouth doughnuts . . . Once again she was jolted by the realization that everything was gone. That pantry and every morsel in it were nothing any more but shapeless cinders and flakes of ash scattered among other cinders and ash.

And Tat? Was there the slightest probability that he was waiting, alive and whole, somewhere along the riverbank for Ellery to claim him? Mary pressed her lips together, hardly feeling the sting where they were cracked and swollen. She would not think of Tat as being like that horse charred on the beach, or the pantry and its contents—or Jewel Collins. Not until she absolutely had to.

"Hush," she said to the whimpering children and to herself. "Crying won't help. We've got to help ourselves."

That sounded like Ma, too. And like Clara. Ma and Clara—she had never recognized the faintest likeness between the two of them before, but the likeness was there. Soft-spoken, gentle Ma and bossy, quick-tempered Clara: neither was one to waste time weeping into her apron. They shared a faculty for facing straight into what had to be faced, each in her own way, with a resolution Mary was not in the least confident she could ever summon.

"Clara?" She touched the quilt as Ellery had done. It might be Clara was asleep. It was difficult to tell with Clara's eyes sealed shut as they were, but Mary risked it, feeling desperately in need of guidance. "Clara?"

Clara moved her head as if it were almost too heavy to manage. "Is Ellery gone?"

"Yes. To find Tat." Mary hesitated. "Aren't you any better? What should I do?"

"Could you—bring me—some water?" Clara's puffed lips made slow work of framing the words.

Water again, and still no means of carrying it. And clearly, no judgments or advice from Clara to be leaned on, either.

"Yes," Mary heard herself promising as firmly as though there were no problem. There had to be a way.

Remembering Mr. Collins's hat, she gave Clara's bonnet an intent study. No, too many little holes burned through it where cinders and sparks must have landed. Perhaps a rag soaked in water and squeezed over Clara's mouth?

"Where you going?" Netty asked, alarmed the instant Mary got painfully to her feet.

"Just to the water to get your mother a drink."

Ida's cravings switched from food to drink. "Firsty. Want water."

"So am I," Netty agreed. "I'm thirsty."

"Come along, then." They, at least, could drink their fill from cupped hands at the river's edge. Mary's only worry would be to keep them from falling in.

Netty scrambled up to follow, but collapsed in a moaning heap after two or three steps. "It hurts. It hurts."

It did hurt. Mary could testify to that. And everything hurt worse for having had a spell of rest in which to stiffen. It hurt enough so that she did not turn back to coax or sympathize, because of the extra steps it would cost.

Ida clamped her fingers around Mary's thumb and trotted beside her to the water's edge. Mary knew a meager gratification, observing how simple it was even to toddle on feet that were undamaged in shoes still all of a piece. Here was proof she had not failed her trust altogether.

And the shoes—"Ida," she said, "how would you like to go barefoot a while?"

Ida had no objections. She worked her bare toes into the sand and ash in evident pleasure at the dry warmth that continued to linger there. Her shoes were sodden from their long wetting, and the leather had gone pulpy, but they did hold water when Mary dipped them in the river. Not a great deal of water, but more than she could hope to carry in cupped hands, and more than could be squeezed satisfactorily from a rag. Whether they leaked some or were only dripping, Mary was uncertain, but in either case, they would serve.

"Here. Now this is a cup and you can have the first drink," she told Ida.

Ida sipped cautiously from the novel cup. "No!" She spat out the water and flung the shoe from her. "Nasty."

Mary made a lunging rescue of the shoe as it was on the brink of falling into the river. "Not nasty. Nice. Look."

She dipped it full again and put it to her own lips. At once she understood. It was as much as she could do not to spit the bad taste from her mouth as violently as Ida had. The water tasted like lye.

Lye, the product of wood ash and water. Last night the ashes of an entire forest had been added to this water.

Well, it was either drink the water as it was or go thirsty. Mary's thirst, now it was aroused, was more insistent than the hunger pangs in her stomach. She ventured a second sip, from the hollow of her hand this time. It went down more readily than the first. Quick gulps, she discovered, tasting as briefly as possible, worked the best, and she contrived to take the edge off her thirst.

Ida, however, would have no part of a second try.

Netty downed the contents of one shoe in a single swallow without a pause to consider the taste or the container. She ran her tongue over her lips to catch every drop, and held the shoe up to Mary. "More?"

"After your mama's had some," Mary said.

Clara made a harder job of finishing her share. She leaned heavily against the support of Mary's shoulder and spilled as much as she sipped, for her swollen lips were awkward.

"Lye. Horrid." She stopped for breath. "But I could drink a barrel."

Mary lost count of the trips she made to the river and back, transporting hardly more water in the ridiculous little shoes than would fill a doll's teacup. After she had limped the distance for the third time, she discarded her own shoes and tore strips from her petticoat to wind around her feet.

She was stilled an instant by the whiteness of her bared feet. Except for sooty smudges of ash that had sifted through the barriers of stocking and shoe, and for the ugly redness surrounding the broken blisters on her soles, the skin was as pale as milk. By contrast, her hands looked as if she had been foolish enough to spend a full day under a broiling sun without wearing gloves. The fear that had lurked in the back of her mind all this endless morning unsteadied her fingers a trifle as she bound her feet in the protective rags and knotted the rag ends around her ankles. She refused to put a name to that fear, though, not until she absolutely had to.

The rags did not reduce the ordeal of walking to and from the river by any considerable amount, but they did protect her raw flesh from being cut deeper by bits of grit and cinder, and that was something. She tore more strips and wet-bandaged Netty's knees when the demand for water slackened. On her last trek to the river, she soaked another, larger piece of petticoat and brought it to lay on Clara's forehead.

"That's good," Clara said in spite of the shivers that continued to sweep her intermittently. "Thank you."

A little later she asked, "Where's Ida?"

"Curled up on your feet," Mary said. "Can't you feel her? I think she's gone to sleep."

"And Netty?"

"Right here. We're all right here but Ellery." Mary paused, pretending to be concentrating on a minor adjustment of the compress, but she might as well have spoken the other missing name. Her silence shouted it louder than her voice: *And Tat.*

Clara shifted under the quilts. "I can't see." She rubbed at her eyes with an impatience that made Mary wince to watch it. "If I could see—"

"Just lie quiet and rest. That's the best you can do. We can handle everything for a while. Ellery can."

"Ellery—" Clara let the word trail off on a sigh.

She lay quiet a time. When she stirred again, her hand came groping out from under the quilt. "Mary?"

Drowsiness was stealing over Mary. She roused herself to slip her hand into Clara's. "Right here."

"The baby," Clara said, barely above a whisper. "I haven't lost it. I was so afraid—the fire, the running, standing so long in the river— But I didn't lose it."

Mary had no answer except to press her sister's hand, and that she had to do gently, mindful of the condition of both her hand and Clara's. *Sisters.* She hadn't ever given thought to the meaning of that word before, beyond chafing against the claim it allowed Clara to have on her. But this was a different Clara, helpless, sick, admitting to fears, appealing for reassurance. *We are sisters.* Mary revolved it in her head as if it were a fact she had only just been told.

"I should have held on," Clara's weak rasp interrupted. "Should never have let go. Not for a second. Knew he'd run if he got the chance, do something crazy if I didn't hang on. He doesn't think ever, just dashes off headlong—"

She was wandering, talking now of Tat, Mary realized. And blaming herself, not Mary.

Something loosened in Mary, like a noose that had been drawing ever tighter. Her breath came suddenly freer. "It's not your fault. You did everything you could possibly do. More. I'm the one he got away from. I'm the one who should have hung on harder. If I'd run faster after him—"

It was Clara's hand that exerted the pressure this time. "Not your fault. Know you did all you could. I knew you would—with the children."

With the children. It was a cough that separated those words from the rest of the speech and lent them a weight that perhaps was not intended, but for Mary, the pause slid the shadow between her and Clara that would always be there to divide them. Clara trusted her fully with her children. But never again with Ellery.

Mary drew her hand free and bent her face into her palms. What wouldn't she give to be able to reassure Clara on that point, too? But it wasn't that simple to banish a person like Ellery from your heart. Not when he filled every chamber of it so completely. What the head said and what the heart did were two different things.

The skin beneath her fingertips was hot as sunburn. Almost without thinking, she spread her fingers across her face, seeking for the silken texture of cheeks and chin she was used to.

Her gasp brought a murmur of concern from Clara. "Mary?"

Mary's fingers were retracing their exploration inch by inch over a surface as stiff and grainy as old leather. She had to explore carefully, for at the same time her face felt like one hot and tender bruise.

The roughness, of course, was her share of the grime she saw coating everyone else. It would soak off when she had the chance to attend to it. She knew it would. Proof was in the charcoal smudge that darkened her fingertip when she rubbed it across her eyebrows . . . Or where her eyebrows used to be. She started to rub again, but was stopped by the smart of scorched flesh.

Her forehead was more like itself up where her bangs had protected it. But the bangs themselves were a thin straggle of wisps punctuated by gaps of uneven stubble. A brush of her hand brought a shower of brittle hair cascading down her face and onto the front of her dress—harsh, discolored fragments of hair that shattered under her fingers.

The rest of her head, with its rich waves of copper that shone gold when she brushed them in sunlight, prodded tufts of short bristles into her fingers. It felt like a loose thatch of oat straw. More strands fell to her shoulders, dislodged by her touch. She dropped her hands to her lap. An entire lock, long, papery and dead, had come away in her hand.

The pound of blood in her ears was so great she thought she might faint.

As from a vast distance, she heard Ida utter a small cry, then Netty's "Papa! Here's Papa!"

When Mary looked up, there Ellery was, standing right above her. She flung herself to her feet and all but into his arms. Never had she so badly needed to be held close and told that everything was going to be all right.

Ellery did not spread his arms to receive her. She swayed off balance, and then quickly squared up her footing. Through her confusion, she belatedly noted that he was alone. Tat was not with him.

"Ellery?" Clara was pushing herself up to sit erect. "Ellery? Mary, is he there?"

Ellery turned and went to his knees beside Clara. "I couldn't find him. I talked to everybody I saw for about a mile down the river, but no one could tell me anything. There are dozens of stray youngsters around, and about twice as many folks out looking for them." He shook his head. "I don't know what to do next. I don't know."

"Papa?" Ida patted his shirt as if she expected a picnic

basket of dainties must be hidden underneath. "Eat?"

"No, baby," he said with a second headshake more weary than the first. "No eat. There's nothing to eat."

"Yes!" Ida insisted. "Eat!" She began to whimper.

"Hush, Ida," Clara said, and coughed. She groped for the little girl and drew her down to her. "Everyone's hungry. We'll have to have water instead."

Another trip to the river for water? Everything—the fear, the grief, the shock, the pain of this day—crystallized for Mary in the thought of having to perform that laborious task one more time. She clenched her fists until the agony of it conquered the scream she felt pushing up through her throat.

"This must be what the war was like," she said in a carefully level voice when she could. It was a straw to cling to, that other people had passed through disaster like this and survived.

"The war? No. There's rules in war. There's a supply line somewhere if a man can get to it. A man knows what he's supposed to do in war, and mostly how to do it. There's orders to carry out, or a plan to follow or an officer around to tell you what to do. I don't know what to do here. I just don't know."

Ellery's tone was aggrieved, his expression baffled, as though he suspected they were the victims of a monstrous trick and he resented it.

A new uneasiness was creeping through Mary. If Ellery saw no hope for them, what chance did they have?

"You asked everywhere about Tat? Everyone? Dark red stockings, that striped shirt—?" Was there a reflection of that same misgiving in Clara's question?

Ellery patted her hand. "Collins and some fellows are going to go through the town later on when they figure the ground's cool enough for them to sift through the ashes. I guess maybe I'll go with them. We can get across the river on what's left of the dam."

Mary bit back an exclamation of protest. Search among the dead before he had looked for Tat everywhere among the living? If there were stray children downriver, why wouldn't there be as many in the other direction where he hadn't really hunted for Tat yet? Or—her uneasiness breathed a chill through her—did he have some knowledge he thought it better not to share with them yet?

"If Tat was here, could we eat?" Netty asked plaintively. "That boy's eating."

Mary's gaze followed Netty's pointing finger to where a man and a trio of boys were crouched around a heap of embers that still glowed dull red. One boy was taking huge bites from something in his hand and appearing to relish every morsel.

Instantly Mary was ravenous. "What is it?"

"Fish," Ellery said. "The river's full of them, floating belly up. I don't know what killed them. The fire some way, I guess."

Mary did not care what killed them, so long as they were edible. "And people are roasting them in the coals? We can do that, too."

If they could drink lye-flavored water, she reflected, they could eat fire-killed fish. She checked herself on the verge of asking why he hadn't mentioned fish sooner. His mind was on Tat, of course. It wasn't fair to expect him to be quite himself while the shock of that loss was still so fresh.

What she did expect was that he would follow her to the river at once. She hobbled to the water's edge and paused. The fish were out there as he had said, dozens of them floating in the current, but none within arm's reach of the bank. If she had looked beyond the shoe in her hand when she had been dipping water, she would have noticed them for herself.

A sudden paralysis gripped her at the thought of having to wade into that cold river again after all the hours she had spent there last night. She turned to see where Ellery was. He had not budged yet from where she had left him, although Netty was rubbing her stomach and crying, and Ida was wailing, "Eat! Eat!"

Something struck Mary's cheek. Another hit the back of her hand and a third splashed down her nose before she could believe what they were: raindrops. Now, twenty-four hours too late, the rain that could have prevented all this was beginning to fall. Rain which, if they wasted much more time, would quench the embers they needed to cook their fish.

"Ellery!" she called in a flare of panic that was very like anger. "Help me!"

A DOZEN OTHER PEOPLE were wading in pursuit of drifting fish bodies when Ellery splashed back to shore, two fair-sized fish in each hand. Eight or ten more men and women were jostling each other around the mound of hot embers that was beginning to steam and sizzle as the raindrops fell faster and closer together.

"You take these and get them started," Ellery told Mary. "I'll see if I can't snare us a couple more."

Mary made her skirt into a basket to receive them. She was ashamed of her display of temper toward him ten minutes ago. His response to her call had been immediate. While she hesitated on the bank, he had plunged straight into the river, even swimming a few strong strokes out in the center to gain one of these fish. It was as if the rain had revived him, restoring him to the Ellery who could handle a half-wild mustang without a flicker of fear or uncertainty.

"Anybody got a knife on him we could use to clean these things?" It was Mr. Collins sloshing ashore with his share of fish in the crown of his long-suffering hat.

"Right here." Ellery slapped his hip and produced a clasp knife from his pocket. "Mary here will be wanting to use it, too."

Mr. Collins peered into Mary's makeshift basket. "Why don't you let me tend to the cleaning and cooking, and maybe you can find a scrap of room for Mrs. Collins under that quilt you were carrying. She's got something of a chill, and she needs some women to talk to."

His nod directed Mary to a woman crouched beside the embers, her hands spread above them as if she were trying to gather warmth.

Mary wished he could have asked on behalf of anyone else, anyone at all but Mrs. Collins. What if she wanted to talk of Jewel? What if she pressed for the gruesome details or berated Mary for not having done something to save Jewel? Mary would far rather have cleaned the fish ten times over than face such an ordeal, but she relinquished her fish to Mr. Collins and walked with him to where his wife crouched.

Mrs. Collins rose at once when he spoke to her. She leaned to inspect the contents of his hat. "What a lot of fish. How glorious. But we can't eat all those ourselves. We'll have to find someone to share them."

"We will," Mr. Collins said. "Some of these belong to the Codys, anyway. I thought you ladies could go sit under Mrs. Cody's quilt out of the rain while the fish are cooking."

"Yes, the rain." Mrs. Collins held out a hand, testing, as if the steady patter of drops on her head and shoulders were not proof enough of the weather's change. Her palm was red from the heat of the coals, but it was smooth and whole. No burns or blisters marred it. Except that she was disheveled and grimy like everyone else, she appeared to have suffered very little damage from the fire physically. "We've prayed so hard and so long, and we need it so badly, it doesn't seem quite right to wish the Lord had picked a more convenient time to send it."

Her eye fell on Mary. "But who is this?"

"I'm Mary James. Clara's sister."

Mrs. Collins smiled at her brightly. "Clara's sister. Of course." The smile became reflective and unfocused. "Such a pretty girl."

Mary flinched inwardly, but at the same time, she had the weird impression that Mrs. Collins was not talking about her, or even to her. Then the moment passed, and Mrs. Collins's gaze was traveling over Mary's scorched and tattered costume with unmistakable interest.

"You were so wise to wear an old dress, my dear," she said, nodding approval. "I wish I'd had your foresight. But who would have guessed what would be most appropriate?"

It was on the tip of Mary's tongue to reply that this was not an old dress, it was her second best, put on yesterday after church to wear for the afternoon. But of course, it was not her second best any more; it was her only dress. Her best dress that she had taken off to spare it from too much wearing, and her oldest dress, which hadn't been nice enough to wear on Sunday, along with her every other garment she was not wearing at this minute, were gone—not saved by being left tidily on a closet hook, but gone. Hadn't Mrs. Collins grasped that fact yet?

Mary glanced up at Mr. Collins, wondering, but his faint shake of the head might have meant anything or nothing. He escorted them to where Clara and the children waited, and helped arrange the two quilts tent fashion over the lot of them. Mrs. Collins chatted on all the while as if she were making agreeable conversation at a church social.

She actually produced a tiny laugh when Mr. Collins left them. "These men probably think we're doing them a kindness, letting them be the campfire cooks. If Mr. Collins only knew how I detest cleaning fish!"

Mary did not envy Mr. Collins his job, either, working out there with no protection from the rain. Neither did she envy Ellery getting soaked further in the river.

Ida and Netty huddled together against her, and she had Clara's head pillowed in her lap. Mrs. Collins sat on the other side of the children, keeping a grip on the uppermost quilt to prevent it from slipping askew. The combined warmth of their bodies under the quilts was not enough to offset the clammy cooling of the atmosphere. Mary wasn't always certain whether the shivers she felt were hers or the children's or Clara's.

The rain was freshening the air, though. The heavy smell of smoke and burned things was slowly thinning. Mary had almost forgotten what it was like to draw a breath that didn't have a sting to it.

Clara was breathing more easily, too. "My head's clearing some," she said. "I think my stomach's quieter."

"Isn't there anything I can do for you?" Mrs. Collins asked. "I wish I'd thought to bring my smelling salts. It's just a shame, you being taken ill out here and in this weather."

A prickle stirred the hairs on Mary's neck. She had dreaded being a witness to Mrs. Collins's grief, to what she had imagined would be wave upon wave of tears and lamentations, but this was worse. There was something eerie about this show of bravery or whatever Mrs. Collins's strange composure was. The things she said wavered on the edge of not making real sense.

Footsteps scuffed nearby, and a man bent to peer under the sheltering quilt. "Mary? Mrs. Cody? Mrs. Collins?"

Mary raised her head. That voice and that lilted accent she would know anywhere. "Sigvard?"

"*Ja*, it's me."

"And you're all right?" She had been so sure he hadn't escaped the flames that the wonder of seeing him squatting in front of her, rain streaming from his dark hair and over his bare shoulders and chest, was very close to joy. To be numbered among the missing, then, did not have to be the same as dead.

"Pretty fair. I got hit in the head by a flying brick when the factory blew up, but it takes more than one brick to dent this thick skull." He grinned, genuinely grinned—a fleeting, sheepish flash of humor that somehow reduced the day's grimness to proportions that could be endured.

"Now I am a peddler." He held up a bundle which, Mary realized, was probably his shirt. "We found a field full of cabbages, every one of them cooked right where it was growing, and we're passing them around as far as the pieces will go."

He handed chunks first to Netty and to Ida, who bit into them and chewed them down without pausing to question or to taste. Mrs. Collins was more dainty in her munching, but Mary, too, found it nearly impossible not to wolf down the wilted, blackened leaves as fast as she could cram them into her mouth.

Clara merely nibbled the edge of her share at first, but the last morsel was gone in nearly as short order as Mary's. "I didn't expect I would be so hungry."

"So many are hungry, and the cabbages are so few," Sigvard said. "It's a pity the pieces couldn't be bigger. For everybody to get some, nobody gets enough." He rose, preparing to leave. "Maybe it will be better soon. I hear that Mr. Mulligan, the boss of the railroad crew, set off a while ago for Marinette to get help."

Marinette. Mary tried to remember what she knew of that place. Seven miles away—wasn't that what Arnold Robinson had told her? What was there to prevent the fire from racing on last night to engulf that town as well?

Mary could not bring herself to ask that question aloud, but there was something she did have to say. "Sigvard, your aunt—"

He nodded. "I know. I found her. It was her heart, I think. *Ja?*"

"I think so. She stayed by me and helped with Ida the whole time we were in the river. Afterward, there was something she wanted me to tell you, but I couldn't make it out, and she couldn't say it plainer. I'm sorry."

"I think I can guess." He pushed aside a dangling lock of wet hair. A bloody crease ran along his temple, no doubt the mark of the brick that had hit him. "The fire closed in too fast. I had to keep running. I couldn't get back. But she wasn't alone." His dark eyes sought and held Mary's. "I thank you for that."

"Your aunt, Sigvard?" Clara turned her swollen face toward him. "I'm very sorry."

"*Ja.*" The low, long-drawn syllable was eloquent of the loss he felt. "She was the same as a mother to me since I was nine." He resettled his grasp on the bundled shirt. "The little one, Tat, Mrs. Cody. Mr. Collins told me. I'll keep an eye out for him."

"And Jewel, too, I hope," Mrs. Collins said, adjusting the drape of the quilt around her shoulder. "She spent last night with a friend. I haven't seen her yet this morning. I suppose she doesn't know exactly where we are."

Again the skin tightened on the nape of Mary's neck, a prickle more sharp this time. Hadn't Mr. Collins told her?

Sigvard cleared his throat. "If I find her, Mrs. Collins, I will be sure to tell you where she is."

"We planned to get over to Mr. Bartels's dry goods store this afternoon to see what material he has suitable for a wedding dress. But now with this rain, I don't know. She's being married in December. Maybe you've heard."

"There isn't any dry goods store any more," Sigvard said, in a way that suggested a man testing the ice one step at a time. "It's all burned up. It's only ashes now. The whole town is gone."

"Yes, the fire," Mrs. Collins sighed. "It took our house. I saw it go." She frowned at him, her chin growing firm. "But by some mercy, Jewel wasn't home last night." In a reflective tone, she added, "I suppose we shall have to send away for the dress goods."

Sigvard and Mary exchanged a look, each questioning the other and accepting the answer. Maybe Mrs. Collins was better off than they were, secure at her muddled picnic, wrapped in cottony layers of confusion against seeing or feeling anything, but it drove a shudder down Mary's spine. To her mind, it was another form of death, and she wasn't sure but what she would prefer to be dead altogether.

Her lips framed a silent "Poor Mr. Collins," and Sigvard's slow nod told her he felt the same. Never before had she been in such accord with another person that there was no need for spoken words to fill in gaps of comprehension. It came on her in a rush that she hadn't thanked him for saving her and Ida, but that, too, she understood in a glance, was a conversation already completed in full without having to be said.

"Well, there are more cabbages to peddle, so many things that must be done." He swung the bundle of cabbage in a kind of salute and turned away.

Mary hugged Netty and Ida closer to her and swallowed the temptation to ask him to stay. How was it that Sigvard Nordquist, of all people, should be the one person with whom she did not feel she was struggling alone against odds that were impossible? Neither did she let herself call after him to know if he would come back when his cabbage was gone. It wouldn't be fair to lay him under such an obligation if, as he said, there was so much else wanting to be done.

She watched the solid breadth of his back, the left shoulder puffed and red from a wide burn, until he was beyond her line of vision. The patter of the rain whispered a curious counterpoint through her head: Ellery declaring, "I just don't know. I don't know what to do."

That wasn't fair, either, she told herself. Ellery was burdened by far heavier responsibilities than Sigvard. No one was dependent on Sigvard but himself. He had no family to worry about. Not any more.

Mrs. Collins was humming under her breath. She began to sing softly: "Showers, showers of blessing, Showers of blessing we need. Mercy drops round us are falling, But for the showers we plead . . . ."

It was the hymn they had sung in church the day Jewel had announced her engagement. Yesterday. Hardly more than twenty-four hours ago.

Mrs. Collins sang it through, every verse and every chorus, four times. She was midway into a fifth rendering when Ellery and Mr. Collins loomed in front of the quilt shelter with their hands and Mr. Collins's hat full of broiled fish.

The fish was still raw inside. Mary did not recall afterward how it tasted, only that she was too hungry to be fastidious beyond the first bleak moment of dismay. Everyone was. The children gulped down each fragment she and Ellery picked free of bones for them and were ready, open-mouthed, for the next like a pair of baby robins. Clara ate the least of all, for her head swam when she sat up and she tended to choke when she tried to swallow lying down. Mrs. Collins ate at her husband's prompting and forgot to finish raising her hand to her mouth whenever he looked away. Nobody had much to say.

"What's that?" Netty asked. Her face paled under its coat of grime. "Papa, I hear something."

"Hear what?" Ellery turned, listening. "There's nothing there. Don't go scaring yourself."

"I hear it. Pounding." Netty shrank beside Ida, terror shaking her.

"Hush," Mary said to calm her. A terror of her own flickered up. What if Netty were to go the way of Mrs. Collins? "Hush. There's nothing to be pounded."

But then she did hear it: a dull thud, thud, like an ax hitting a stake. It was some distance off, a pulsation in the atmosphere behind the wailing of a baby here and there and the scattering of cries, coughs, and calling voices that seemed to have been going on forever. Or was there a subtle change in the tone of the voices?

"By thunder," Mr. Collins said, "I do believe—"

He and Ellery stood up together.

"There!" Ellery pointed. "It looks like— It is. They're putting up a tent."

A tent! It came over Mary in a wave how cold and wet and thoroughly miserable she was. The shelter of a tent sounded like the first step into heaven.

"I see wagons, too. Three, four, maybe more," Mr. Collins said. "That Mulligan fellow must have got through to Marinette. Which means Marinette's still there."

"Come on. Let's see what's doing." Ellery was already launching into his stride.

"Wait! Wait!" Mary's disappointment was too great to be contained. "Can't we go, too?"

He stopped short and turned a blank face to her as if the thought were one he had to puzzle through. "Why, yes, I suppose so. Or we'll come back for you—"

He was curious to learn what was happening, impatient to be off. Like a little boy, Mary thought, and for no reason she could name, she wanted to cry. Did he imagine there was something homelike about this desolate stretch of riverbank that they would be in no hurry to leave? She was so tired of explaining and urging.

An ally rose up from a surprising quarter.

"No, we must be going," Mrs. Collins said, getting to her feet. She stooped to brush at the hopeless layer of ash and dirt on her skirt as she might have a sprinkling of cake crumbs after a tea. "If others are leaving, we needn't worry that we haven't stayed long enough."

Other people were indeed leaving, Mary saw, when she wrestled Ida and Netty up and out from under the folds of quilt that Mrs. Collins's rising had collapsed on them. By straggling twos and threes, or stumbling along alone, they were moving in the same direction, toward the pounding. Everyone who could command the strength to move.

Mary bent to Clara, whose head still rested in Mary's lap. "Did you hear, Clara? Help's coming. There's a tent and some wagons. We'll be all right if we can get to them."

Clara understood. "I can walk, I think. A tent—? I can walk."

She did gain her feet, sitting a while first, taking shallow breaths and leaning against Mary before letting Ellery raise her the rest of the way. There she stood swaying, clinging to his arm with both her own.

"Go on," she panted. "If we don't stop, if we just keep going, I think I can make it."

Netty hobbled a few steps and began to cry. Mr. Collins picked her up. Mary started to lift Ida, but the pain that broke through her stiffened shoulder forced her to set the baby down quickly before she dropped her.

"I can't carry you," Mary said on a near sob. She held out her hand. "But you can walk with me."

"No." Ida stretched her arms above her head. "Ca'y me."

There was a chuckle from Mrs. Collins. "A mind of her own. That's just like our Jewel at that age. Let me carry her if she doesn't care to walk."

They formed as halting and slow a procession as any along the river. Mary heaped the two quilts up in her good arm as well as she could and brought up the rear. The quilts were wet and filthy and riddled with burn holes, but she couldn't bring herself to abandon them on the chance that the tent would provide blankets that were clean and whole.

She marveled at the endurance Ellery and the Collinses appeared to have. And Clara, too. Gradually it became the only thing that drew her onward. A bone-deep weariness was soaking into her like the rain to where even the torment in her burned feet was dulled. The rags she had wrapped around her feet shifted and loosened, and she remembered Ida's shoes and the remnants of her own. They had been left behind, forgotten, on the riverbank, but nothing in the world could have turned her back to plod the tedious distance to retrieve them, although they were the only excuse for foot covering she and Ida had.

Then Clara fell. She went down without a whisper of warning and without a gesture to save herself. Ellery caught her before she struck the ground. He lowered her carefully the rest of the way, and she lay motionless as a mound of discarded rags.

"Mother!"

Mary heard in his voice the fear that was hers. "No!" she cried so fiercely that it hurt her throat, but the hot taste of tears was in her mouth as she flung herself forward to kneel at her sister's side.

Ellery had one of Clara's hands, pressing it between both his own. "Is she—"

"No," Mary repeated. "No, no, no."

She lifted Clara's other hand, feeling for a pulse. An irrational dread seized her that if they lost Clara they would lose everything. The tent and its promise of rescue would retreat forever beyond their reach.

Clara's hand stirred. The fingers curved to touch Mary's. "Can't," she breathed. "I—can't."

"You can. You can." Mary used her sleeve to blot the beads of moisture from Clara's forehead that might have been raindrops or perspiration. "We'll carry you."

To prove it, she slipped her arm beneath Clara's head. Bad shoulder or not, she felt capable of doing anything if she had to.

"I'll carry her," Ellery said. He shifted his position, gathered himself, and with a heave, rose to his feet, Clara cradled in his arms.

But Clara was not a small woman. She was built solidly on a large frame, and she was not supple at the best of times. Big with child as she was now, and too spent to be much less than a dead weight, she was an awkward burden for one man to handle, even as splendid a man as Ellery. He clamped her against him, bending her nearly double, and lurched onward, leaning into the rain as though he were facing into a gale.

Mary struggled up from her knees. She had to help in the carrying. It was almost certain that, unaided, he would stumble sooner or later, and he and Clara would go crashing to earth together.

Then there were two men beside him. They had an improvised litter made out of a blanket fastened to a pair of poles, and they were lifting Clara onto it and bearing her off toward the tent.

For a dazed moment, Mary merely stared after them. Men with eyebrows and full beards and fully clad in rough wool shirts and trousers and heavy boots, they looked strangely alien among the scarecrow survivors of Peshtigo. Never in her life had she seen a man without his shirt, not her father nor her brothers. Yet this day, everywhere she chose to turn, there were men, women, and children so close to being naked that the distinction was too fine to be argued. Her only reaction was to wonder at how unremarkable it all seemed.

Yes, and at how beautiful these loggers from Marinette were.

She started running to catch up to them and Ellery and

Clara. Tears she had been unaware of blurred her vision. She tripped and went down on her hands and knees.

Someone was beside her, lifting her up. "It's all right. There's no hurry."

He was a stocky, red-bearded man in the rough, yellow coveralls that were pratically the uniform of men who worked in the sawmills. "Here now, drink this. Maybe it will help." He pressed a tin cup into her hand. "Careful. Hold it by the handle. It's hot."

It was coffee, strong and sweet and radiating heat. She could trace the descent of its warmth through her as she sipped. She sipped only because it was too hot to gulp.

"Thank you," she gasped when she had tilted the cup to get the last delicious drop.

He collected the fallen quilts for her and slid a steady hand beneath her elbow to propel her forward. "There's plenty more. Food, too: fried chicken, beef, ham, cheese, bread. We've been fighting fires in the west end of Marinette all night, but they're out now, and when we heard what had happened down here, the ladies in town just about emptied out their larders."

"My sister—Clara—" Mary waved the cup vaguely in the direction in which the men had borne Clara off.

"They'll be taking her to the tent. That's where you want to go, too, until we can get the wagons ready to take you back to Marinette. They're setting up a hospital in the Dunlap House there."

Mary surrendered to the simplicity of being looked after, of letting someone else do the thinking, the deciding, the providing. In a short time she was the stronger for a second cup of coffee and a massive sandwich into which the logger in charge of the food had crammed every good thing at his disposal.

She soon discovered that there was little advantage to being inside the tent except that it kept off the rain. The ground here was as damp to sit on as the riverbank, and the rank smell of wet ashes and smoke trapped within the walls was sickening.

She found Clara lying close to a side wall, Netty and Ida and Mrs. Collins huddled beside her. Neither Ellery nor Mr. Collins was with them.

"Papa's gone to look for Tat," Netty volunteered. She was chewing the meat from a drumstick while Ida sat sucking on the bone of another. Someone had wrapped Ida's blistered hand in a man's red bandanna.

"We got to drink coffee," Netty added. "Did you get some?"

"Yes."

Mary was casting about her for space in which to spread out the quilts, but there was not room enough. She compromised by folding one under Clara's head for a pillow and wadding the other behind herself as a backrest against which she could lean her throbbing shoulder. Mrs. Collins was humming softly to herself, lost in contemplations of her own.

"Mary," Clara said. Her hand groped outward and Mary took it. Clara was not questioning, only seeking an acknowledgment of Mary's presence.

The space within the canvas walls was rapidly shrinking. More and more people dragged themselves inside or were carried in. Some were so horribly burned that she could not bear to look at them. It was hardly possible that they could still be alive. If Tat were among them, she might not know him. Worse, if Tat were one of them, she wasn't sure she could bear to know.

She tried to watch instead the rescuing loggers as they supported stumbling victims, fetched coffee and food, and did what they could to ease the suffering around them. They were kindness itself, these brawny woodsmen who brawled and drank and sinned so outrageously on other occasions that it was said a decent woman dared not walk down the street.

One of the loggers paused in front of her. "It won't be much longer and we'll have you folks on your way to where they can do something for those burns." He brushed a calloused hand across the top of Netty's head. "Just hang on a little while more."

Mary smiled her thanks at him, ignoring for the moment the angry heat a change of expression revived in her stiffening cheeks. Pleased surprise had always been the male reaction to a special Mary James smile, but this man's eyes merely skimmed over her face and slid away. He nodded quickly and moved on. It was as if what he saw had made him uncomfortable.

Mary sat like something chiseled from stone, except for the spinning in her mind. "Ellery! Ellery!" she was silently screaming through the tent walls to wherever he was. "Take me out of here. Take me away. Please, somebody. Please!"

It was the red-bearded mill hand who stooped above her to offer his help when the time came to get into the wagons. "Maybe if we get you aboard first, you and the little ones can help cushion this lady here," he said, indicating Clara.

Clara stirred as if she were rousing from a doze. "Ellery—?"

"I don't know who he is, ma'am," the man said, "but there'll be more wagons later for those that can't fit in these. The folks who can manage to walk can follow along behind."

A fresh panic spread through Mary. Must they leave without Ellery? They couldn't undergo another separation. And what was she to do, alone in a strange town with Clara unable to make decisions and no one else to turn to?

The red-bearded man was explaining it all again to Mrs. Collins, how those most in need of medical attention must go first and the others must wait a while. "I can't go off to Marinette in any case," Mrs. Collins agreed. "My daughter doesn't even know I'm here. She'd never think to look for me in Marinette."

Poor Mrs. Collins, Mary thought automatically, and then wondered if the woman were not more to be envied than pitied.

Mary let herself be half-led, half-carried to one of the wagons. She settled herself in a corner, the two children nestled next to her. Clara came, limping the short distance with the aid of a sturdy logger on each side. They helped her into the wagon where she could lie with her head once more pillowed in Mary's lap. Mary lost count of how many others were crowded in beside them before the wagon could hold no more.

The driver was preparing to climb up to his seat when Netty said, "There's Papa."

Ellery came scuffing through the debris and ashes to stand alongside the wheel, peering in at them. There was no need to ask if he had found Tat. He was alone, but relief flooded

Mary's heart all the same. "Are you coming with us?"

"Ellery?" Clara struggled to raise her head. "Have you heard any word? Has anyone seen Tat?"

"No. None of the folks that have been coming up here to the tent. I haven't got any farther." He paused to drink from the cup of coffee he held. "It didn't burn more than half a mile east of town. Some fellows walked up here from the harbor a while ago. The sawmill, the warehouse, the docks down there, nothing was touched."

"But our side—" Clara's voice caught on a cough, but she forced it on. "Our side of the river?"

"There's folks over there that made it through. Somebody's brought up a boat to help bring them across. Collins went over the first chance he got, but I thought—" Ellery shook his head slowly, studying the rim of his cup. "I guess I'll wait here a spell longer and see."

Wait? What was there to gain by waiting? Mary pressed her fingertips to her eyes in a futile effort to clear her vision for a sharper look at him through the misting rain. Wasn't knowing for certain, if there were any way to know, better than existing in a torment of unanswered hope and fear? Yes, even if in the end the knowing must be finished like Mr. Collins's among the ashes of French Street? If nothing else, the knowledge would have let them all stay together.

"Papa?" Ida shrilled as the driver clucked to the team and the wagon jolted forward. She stretched her arms toward Ellery before doubling up in a fit of wheezing, gasping coughs.

"It's all right." Ellery kept step with them for a few paces, reaching in to pat Ida's bent shoulders, to touch Clara's cheek.

"I'll be along when I can. But you're in good hands now. It's all right."

He stepped aside out of the path of the rear wheel and let the wagon move on by. When Mary straightened again from her attempts to help Ida regain her breath, the tent had grown smaller and he had turned away. He dwindled to an oddly unimposing figure wandering aimlessly through the rain as the wagon creaked and jounced in search of a road that had been erased.

A thin, despairing cry wavered above the normal sounds of Marinette's Dunlap House, the hotel turned hospital for the victims of the fire. The cry was cut short by the closing of a door down the hall.

Mary, her chair turned to catch the afternoon light on her sewing, did not raise her head. Her fingers were awkward, and it took concentration to keep her hold on the needle, let alone work it through the fabric in the neat, small stitches she had been taught by Ma. Dr. May, who had come north from Fond du Lac to operate this makeshift hospital, had said that she must use her hands as much as possible or the red scar tissue that was replacing her blisters of three weeks ago would leave her nothing but stiffened claws. Besides, in these past three weeks she had grown accustomed to hearing strange calls and cries at almost any time of day or night.

It was Clara who started in response to the sound. "What?"

Her head jerked up from the pillow. She struggled up on one elbow in the bed.

"Nothing," Mary said. "Just Mrs. Holst having one of her spells, I think."

Mrs. Holst was an elderly German woman, whose entire family—husband, sons, daughter, daughter-in-law and grandchildren—had been lost in the fire. No one seemed to know which particular horror it was that had stopped time for her, but for her the fire raged endlessly on by day and by night whether she slept or was awake.

"I guess I was dozing," Clara said.

She pushed the pillow higher for a backrest and settled the green eyeshade over her forehead more firmly. Most of the swelling had left her face, and little by little her sight was returning, but Dr. May wanted her to put no undue strain on her eyes for several weeks to come. Neither did he want her out of bed and moving around any more than was necessary before the baby arrived.

Several days ago, a second hospital had been opened, this one attached to the Merryman Hotel, to relieve the crowding at the Dunlap House, but there had been no question of transferring Clara. Therefore, Mary and Netty and Ida were still here, too, because there was nowhere else for them to go.

"I thought it was Tat calling me," Clara said to the heavy Army blanket that covered her. "I'm always thinking that I hear him somewhere."

Mary nodded. "I know. I think I do, too, sometimes."

It wasn't only Mrs. Holst who was haunted. They all had their personal ghosts and nightmares that pounced on them during sleep or whenever they relaxed their guard too far.

For Mary it was that slow, bumping ride from the ruins of Peshtigo to Marinette. She had barely to close her eyes to see again mile upon empty, charred mile of what had been forest, the black boles of once-giant trees still upright here and there like the broken pillars of a demolished castle. The bodies of animals—deer, bear, cattle, and smaller creatures—littered the ash-strewn road, some still recognizable for what they had been, some mere suggestive cinders and fragments of bone. Everything was black, burned, dead.

As a reality, that journey had been nightmare enough. As a dream that stole on her while she slept and held her captive for an eternity almost every night, it was far worse. It was the feeling that terrified her more than the landscape: the sensation that she was alone, utterly and unalterably cut off and alone. Clara and Ida and Netty were with her, but they were inert forms, helpless even to brace themselves against the jolting of the wagon without her aid. No one else occupied the wagon except the hazy figure of the driver, who kept his back to them and never spoke. There was only Mary to do anything that must be done, and there was nothing that she could do because of something irrevocable she had already done.

Mary pressed her lips against dwelling further on the dream. The best way to defeat it was to think of something else.

She thrust her needle to and fro in a trio of final, fastening stitches, and snipped off the thread. "There." She held up the garment, a child's dress of yellow velvet, and gave it a shake. "This would be nicer if I had an iron to run over it, but at least she won't be tripping on it, and most of that stain at the bottom got turned up out of sight in the new hem. Come here, Netty, and try it on."

Netty left the corncobs she and Ida were lining up along the window sill, pretending they were dolls. Obediently, she raised her arms to have the yellow dress slipped down over her head and buttoned up the back. It went on smoothly over the skimpy brown pinafore she was already wearing.

"Good." Mary patted the dress at the shoulders and tugged a little on the skirt, then sat back to admire her handiwork. "That brown thing can serve for a petticoat from now on. Stockings, shoes, petticoat, dress: you're a regular princess for these parts, Netty."

"Princess, indeed," Clara said, while Netty giggled and slid her hands along the skirt folds, petting the material. "Imagine! Yellow velvet for a five-year-old."

"Velvet is warm, though. It's practical from that point of view."

Mary worked the needle into a scrap of paper to help prevent its being lost, and tucked it, her thimble, and the scissors into a small drawstring bag. All these items were loans to her from one of the women doing nursing at the hospital, and they were as precious as jewels.

"Besides," she added, "beggars can't be choosers. Some in rags, some in tags, and some in velvet gowns, you know."

Since word of Peshtigo's disaster had reached the outer world, every steamer that put in to Marinette from Green Bay had brought donations of blankets and clothing for the fire victims. A disappointing number of the contributions, however, were better testimony to the givers' good intentions than to their common sense.

It was odd how being destitute altered one's values. Mary had lingered only briefly over a hat of exquisite silk roses and a ball gown of frothy blue tulle embroidered with gold thread, before bearing off in triumph a pair of flannel petticoats—one set for her and one set for Clara—and a simple gray wool dress that looked as if it had belonged first to a Quaker. The weather since the fire had been growing steadily cooler, and the donations most prized were those that took into account that the northern winter was not far off.

Clara stretched her arm to finger the row of tucks Mary had stitched to bring a semblance of fit to the flannel dress Ida was wearing. "Rags and tags is pretty much what we'd have if it were left up to me. I can sew if I have to, but I don't have your gift for turning a rag into a dressmaker's creation with just a few snips and a needle. Don't have the patience for it, either. I believe I'd rather scrub floors."

Praise from Clara, even indirect praise, was such a rarity that Mary was as much embarrassed by it as pleased.

She knelt to grope under the bed for the pasteboard box one of the nurses had bestowed on her the other day to hold what few possessions the Codys had acquired since the fire. "Ma says everyone has at least one talent. Maybe sewing is mine."

She reflected on the green dress she had put together with so much pride just before she left home for Peshtigo. That beautiful green dress, designed to set off to perfection a beautiful girl—both of them gone now, forever.

Many of the Dunlap House furnishings had been moved into temporary storage to make room for more beds, but enough mirrors remained around and about that a person not confined to bed could hardly avoid seeing herself—especially a person who was prone from lifelong habit to glance into any mirror she passed. Mary was beyond the stage of being shocked by the sorry creature that stared back at her from within each mirror frame. She doubted that she would ever grow used to accepting that creature as herself. The angry red would gradually fade from her skin, Dr. May had said, and bit by bit the crusty texture of her complexion would soften away. (He had not said that her face would ever again be petal smooth and fresh.)

In time, of course, her hair would grow back. It was cropped shorter than a boy's now, in an attempt to even up the scorched and broken patches and minimize the stubble. But it would be years before it could regain its former length, if it ever did. As for the luster and thickness of which she had once been so proud—she was learning not to look in mirrors if she could avoid it, and, with greater difficulty, trying not to care.

"I wonder about those children at the church," Clara said, turning her face, blinking, away from the strong light of the window. "Someone's seeing to it that they're decently dressed, I suppose, and not in just the leavings after the rest of us have helped ourselves."

That wasn't really what she was wondering, and Mary knew it. Children orphaned by the fire were being housed in a barracks behind the Presbyterian church until they could be claimed by relatives or other arrangements made for them.

Clara had dispatched Ellery on at least a dozen fruitless missions there on the chance that Tat might one day be among the thinning trickle of strays that continued to be brought in by people who had found and befriended them. She clung to a belief that Tat was alive somewhere almost as tenaciously as Mrs. Collins did to her delusion that Jewel was not dead.

"I was thinking I might take a short walk this afternoon," Mary said, without having thought anything of the kind until this moment. "Ellery says the church isn't far from here. Maybe I'll stop and see what it's like."

"Would you? I know your feet are still tender, but if you think you could manage it—" Clara gave a twitch to the bedclothes that sent a misplaced corncob doll bounding to the floor. "If only I had the use of my legs! Ellery's been so busy scouting the boardinghouses and whatnot for a place where we can live this winter that he hasn't been in to see those children since Wednesday."

"I'll do fine, as long as I don't have to worry about you. You sit still and behave yourself."

Mary drew a voluminous shawl and a knitted stocking cap from the box. Once she wouldn't have been caught dead in such a ridiculous costume, but the cap and shawl were true treasures now, although she couldn't help a wry grin as she tugged the cap down over her shorn head. "Just in case you suspect my real purpose is to dazzle the handsome loggers of Marinette and forget my errand, I'll take Netty along to keep me on the straight and narrow."

She was rewarded by a squeak of assent from Netty and a passable chuckle from Clara. "You'll garner second looks at any rate, I'll warrant that," Clara said. "Ida, bring your corncob dollies here on the bed, and you and Mama will figure out what their names are."

Netty scrambled to don the wraps that had fallen to her lot: a patched but still sturdy jacket and a worn beaver bonnet that must once have belonged to a wealthy child. She had become Mary's shadow during these hospital weeks when her mother was confined to bed and her father was a restless now-and-then visitor.

Her hand slid into Mary's as they worked their way out of the room, pausing at each of the other beds crowded into it to pick up a fallen pillow or smooth a twisted blanket or fill a tumbler of water. Mary paused at several of the doors along the hall as well to call a greeting here, relay a message there. It was a habit she had formed after her burns were healed enough for her to be up and around. There were dozens of small services to be done for the patients less fortunate than she, and nowhere near the number of hands required to do them all. Keeping herself busy prevented her from brooding too deeply on her own misfortune. The crippling and scars and pain she witnessed everywhere bore in on her again and again that by comparison she was indeed one of the fortunate ones. It was also a heartening revelation to discover herself welcomed by smiles and brightened expressions despite her damaged face.

How she would be accepted outside the hospital, however, was a different matter. The veranda of the Dunlap House was as far as she had ventured until now, not altogether because of the condition of her feet. She wasn't sorry to have Netty's trusting hand to squeeze as they descended the stairs to the lobby.

"There's Papa!" Netty exclaimed. She pointed to a knot of men talking near the door, but she didn't break her hold on Mary's hand to run ahead to him.

Mary had no need of the pointer. Ellery's fair head as always rose above the others around him. Besides that, he was garbed in a matching blue coat and trousers from the Army stores President Grant had ordered sent north from Chicago to aid the survivors. Never mind that the coat wasn't large enough for him and tended to bunch across the shoulders. Amid the motley costumes of the other men, he was a figure that even the most casual glance could not help but single out.

Would there ever be a day, Mary wondered, when a glance of hers in Ellery's direction would truly be casual? Her feelings toward him these days were such a jumble that she was no longer sure what they were, except that the old easiness between them was gone. She would have been glad if she and Netty could have slipped past the group unnoticed, but that, of course, was impossible.

Discomfort betrayed her into abruptness when Ellery turned and nodded to acknowledge their approach.

"I thought you were away this afternoon," she said, "checking on making room for us to stay in a cabin or a little house or something."

"There's still time. I'm going soon." A lift of his shoulder dismissed the matter as if it were of no real importance or else as good as accomplished.

But neither was the fact, Mary knew. The Dunlap House couldn't and undoubtedly wouldn't continue to house them forever once none of them was in need of daily medical attention. From what she had heard, any kind of shelter that provided four walls and a roof was in demand for homes for Peshtigo's homeless families.

The fire had raged northward for over sixty miles that night, cutting a swath of destruction fifteen miles wide at times and rarely leaving more than the blackened stones of a cellar or a few charred timbers where a dwelling had been. No lives had been lost in Marinette, but the town had not escaped untouched. Upward of a dozen buildings on the town's west side, one of them a boardinghouse, had burned to the ground. Others had been damaged, adding to the shortage of housing.

Barns, sheds, stables, lofts—any livable quarters whatever—were being pressed into service as quickly as it was known they were available. Twice in recent days Ellery had gone to look over possible accomodations, only to find another family—in one case, three families—already settling themselves in to stay.

Mary bit back the impulse to urge him to hurry this time. More than once lately she had caught herself on the brink of prompting him to do this or to remember that, as if she were his mother rather than a girl half his age. Or as if she had somehow stepped into the shoes Clara wasn't yet strong enough to wear.

She smoothed her hand over the silky fur of Netty's bonnet, not looking at him, and changed the subject. "Well, we're going for a walk to show off our finery. Netty's got a new dress."

"Very pretty," Ellery said.

Netty beamed her pleasure, although it was difficult for

Mary to believe his indifferent glance had marked so much as the velvet's color. He seldom let his eyes linger on either of his children these days, or on anyone else, Mary realized. His gaze seemed always to drift a fraction to the right or left.

"You come, too, Papa?" Netty invited. "We're going by the orphans."

Ellery's brow creased. He shook his head. "Not today. Papa has other things to do."

Mary wondered if his answer would have been the same had their destination been somewhere else. He never spoke of Tat if he could avoid it. His search for the little boy among the ashes of Peshtigo had been in vain, and she suspected that he had long given up hope that they would ever learn more of Tat's fate than they knew right now. Over a thousand people had died in the fire, men, women, and children. Three hundred and fifty of them, charred past recognition, were buried in a mass grave, their names forever lost.

"We turn right at the corner, don't we, to find the church?" Mary asked. "Or is it left?"

"I'm going that way," a man behind Ellery spoke up. "I can show you, if you don't mind company."

"Sigvard!" Mary stared, then laughed at her own astonishment. "You're so splendid, I didn't recognize you."

He had been a visitor at the hospital a handful of times to have his burns dressed and to stop by for a word with her and Clara, but when she had last seen him, he was wearing a pair of shapeless trousers, a logger's red shirt, and boots cracked along the seams. These were still the foundation of his costume, she saw, but they were topped today by a magnificent swallowtail coat that might well have graced the back of a gentleman at a society function in New York or Chicago.

"Well, I thought I'd soon be needing a coat, so I took the first one in the barrel that didn't choke me and that looked like it might last the winter." Sigvard grinned and turned for her to see the tall silk hat he held. "I got a chimney here, too, to keep my head warm when it snows."

Another of the men chuckled. "You better stick to crop raising on that new farm. No respectable horse or cow's going to let you in whistling range wearing that getup."

Sigvard gave the coat tails a jaunty flip. "It'll be good for keeping the crows scared out of the corn."

He opened the door for Netty and Mary and followed them outside.

"What is this about a new farm?" Mary asked as they started along the sidewalk. "Are you leaving us?"

The idea left a curiously hollow feeling in her. Many people were leaving, of course. Mr. and Mrs. Collins were departing on the next steamer up from Green Bay, their destination the home of Mr. Collins's brother in Galena, Illinois. Mrs. Collins, fretting over Jewel's delay in returning from that overnight visit, was still murmuring of wedding gowns and wedding plans. Even Ellery had spoken of leaving, of moving elsewhere to start over, although where that would be or what he would do or how they would get there were vague.

But Sigvard she had come to look on as a fixture. For one thing, he seemed always to be occupied, never at loose ends as Ellery and a good share of the other men often were. He had stayed at Peshtigo to help gather up the dead, had aided in the construction of coffins from rough pine boards supplied by the mill at the mouth of Peshtigo Harbor, which had been miraculously spared by the flames, and had done his part in digging countless graves. A few days ago he had mentioned he might sign on with one of the logging crews that would be spending the winter harvesting what lumber they could from the burned-over land before the damaged wood fell prey to pine borers—worms that would eat away a neglected log or ailing tree from the inside. She was disappointed at the thought that he was ready to quit the area altogether, that he would be gone and she would not.

Sigvard contrived to shrug as he settled the tall hat firmly over his dark, thick hair. "It's a farm in the Middle Sugar Bush, sixty acres about three miles out of Peshtigo. The owner's offered to deed it over to me if I want it. He's moving his family back to Oshkosh where they came from."

"Why?" Mary asked.

"It's burned off, the farm is. Buildings, everything gone. And he thought for a while some of his family was lost, too. They only came up here last year."

Mary shook her head. It was an odd sensation without the accompanying swish of silken hair she was used to. "I meant, why deed it to you?"

Sigvard pondered the answer in that slow way of his that had once so infuriated her. She had greater patience now, and more respect for the mind operating behind the manner she had been too quick to label stupidity.

Her own mind did a sudden leap. "That boy you ran after when we were almost to the river that night, you and your aunt and Ida and I, remember? What became of him? Did you get to him in time? Did he ever find his family?"

"*Ja*." Sigvard reached down to take the hand Netty shyly slipped into his. "*Ja* to all three questions. We didn't find his folks until it was daylight, but they were together and in good shape, even the grandma. And he was okay with me all night in the river."

"Is it his father who wants to deed you the farm?"

"No." Sigvard's dark eyes held a twinkle as they met hers and deflated her pride in her shrewdness. "But it's something like that. There was a little girl like Netty here, fell between two logs and was pinned down. Her father couldn't move them apart by himself, but together we got her out. He's the farmer from Oshkosh that wants to go back."

Two children rescued and returned to their families. Herself and Ida turned from a burning street and guided to the river. How many others had he helped, Mary wondered. There was more to the farm story, she was sure, but she was no less sure that she would have to probe and prompt beyond the bounds of common decency to extract the full account from him. Sigvard saw nothing extraordinary in giving what help he could where it was needed. He would probably be astounded if not actually indignant if she were to suggest that he was a hero.

She squeezed the hand Netty entrusted to her as they waited at the edge of the plank walk for a team and wagon to rattle past the corner. "You'll accept the farm, won't you? Didn't you once say that was what your aunt and uncle always wanted for you?"

"It is what they wanted, true. But I don't know. I have to think. A farm is too much to take for a gift. I would want to pay a fair price . . ." A negative bob of the tall hat dismissed the chance of his soon being able to do that.

Mary could have argued that an unwanted farm wasn't such an impossible exchange for a little girl's life, but something in her was pleased that he didn't see it that way. Farming, however, was a subject she did know a little about. "It can't be worth near as much now as it was before: a burned-out farm, no buildings, no seed, no tools, no stock, no pasturage, no wood. Someone told Ellery the grass roots were killed, and that the fire even followed the tree roots down into the ground and left holes where they used to be. It'll take time and a lot of work to make a real farm again out of land like that. Not everybody's going to want to try."

"I'm not afraid of hard work." Sigvard flexed his shoulders under the fine black cloth of his coat. Incongruous though the elegant garment was against a background of sawdust-paved streets and wooden sidewalks splintered by the spikes of loggers' heavy boots, its effect was to mark the compact yet supple strength of his silhouette.

He was lost in thought for the length of half a block. At last he said, "There will be some money from working in the woods this winter. And there's the money my aunt was saving for the farm." He gave Mary a thin smile. "That's what she was trying to have you tell me, I think: that those savings got left behind at the house and everything was gone. But when I went back where the house had been, the box was still under the stone where she kept it and every penny was still there."

His smile was clouded by the shadow that nearly always crossed his face when he spoke of matters relating to his aunt's death. That was one reason, perhaps, for his reluctance to speak much of his rescues that night, Mary thought; he would forever regret not having been at his aunt's side through those final hours. Circumstances, not deliberate choice, had decreed how things must be. But this was salve that had small power to heal. Mary's sympathy went out to him from the soreness of her own guilt.

"And then there's your blacksmithing," she said to distract him. "There must be plenty of smith's work to be had here. I've seen two buggies, a carriage, and a wagon go by us in just one block."

"The blacksmith trade, that is part of the trouble. It's good work. I like it, making things, mending them. Maybe it will be a hard thing to give up."

"Couldn't you do both? Work the farm and run a forge? At home my Pa cobbles shoes in the winter after the farm work's done."

Sigvard's steps slowed as he considered. "I could, couldn't I?" He gave the hat brim a contemplative tug that set the hat at a jauntier angle. "Maybe I will think more before I decide."

"At least you won't have to spend time on cutting trees to clear the fields." Mary bent her head to smile up at him in a gesture that might once have been thought coquettish. In reality it was an excuse to avert her face from the curious gaze of two women driving by in a pony cart. That same curiosity had been on too many of the other faces that had looked toward her from the buggy and carriage and wagon seats.

She didn't mind the friendly smiles provoked by the donated clothing. The makeshift costumes were amusing, after all, and they were also in their way a badge of triumph, a proclamation of survival. But when the smiles lifted to her face and faded to compassion as the women's in the pony cart had done, or vanished into blankness as the wagon driver's had, a prickling dampness that was anything but triumphant broke out along her hairline.

Her mistake had been to forget that people outside the hospital would not have had their shock blunted by the daily sight of dozens of faces as cruelly sand-scoured and heat-ravaged as hers or worse. She had forgotten, too, that complexions could be as creamy pale and delicately tinted as those of the young women in the cart. A quick look had assured her that they were neither of them remarkable in any other respect. But what did it matter with lovely, fresh skin that had obviously never been exposed to the out-of-doors without the protection of a parasol or veil and deep-brimmed bonnet?

"*Ja,* that is so. The land is cleared." Sigvard chuckled, paying no heed to passing traffic.

It was Netty who suddenly hung back and twisted to gaze after the cart.

"Netty, come on," Mary urged, in no humor to linger. "What are you doing?"

"Cabbages." Netty pulled her hand free from Sigvard's and pointed. "They got cabbages."

Mary darted a wary glance behind her. A market basket sat in the back of the cart, and a cabbage was indeed perched atop the other contents.

"You're right," she told Netty. "They've got a cabbage. What about it?"

"There's babies under cabbages," Netty said. "Papa says he'll find me a baby brother soon. One just like Tat."

Mary lowered her eyes to avoid any chance encounter with

Sigvard's. Birth and expected babies were not fitting topics for discussion in the presence of a young man. She was uncertain whether to laugh or to pretend deafness—or to examine further a stab of dismay that was more than mere embarrassment.

"Not all cabbages have babies under them," Sigvard said, as if it were as routine a subject as the weather. "And sometimes what you find is a baby sister, not a brother. You have to take what you find, and you don't know what that is until you get there."

"My Papa knows." Netty's confidence was not in the least shaken. "He's going to get us another brother because he can't find Tat."

For an instant, Mary's dismay sharpened to a spurt of anger. How could Ellery make such a statement? It wasn't fair. Especially it wasn't fair to Clara. It was the same as saying that all these months of care and pain, these weeks of anxious waiting, would be wasted effort if the baby were a girl. And if the baby were a boy, were they then to forget about Tat? Forget that Tat had ever been?

Sigvard recaptured Netty's hand, drawing her onward. "Well, some cabbages are just for eating, not for babies. I think we'll have to wait for your Papa to find the right one."

Mary could think of nothing to say. The old litany of "If only's" was repeating itself in her mind: If only she had held tighter to Tat. If only she had run faster after him. If only she and Clara hadn't quarreled so bitterly that day. If only she had tried a little harder to be civil from the start.

"*The Lord hath afflicted me in the day of His fierce anger.*"

She had overheard a visitor to the hospital telling someone

that this was part of the text of the sermon preached last Sunday by Marinette's Lutheran minister against the sinful, pleasure-seeking, boisterous frontier immorality of Peshtigo. The verse had haunted her ever since, like a spectral finger pointing directly at her.

It was not much farther to the corner of Newberry, where the Presbyterian church stood just off Main Street. Behind the church sprawled a long, one-story building of unpainted pine boards. It housed the fire orphans and several homeless families as well as a community dining hall where those who had no place else to go could eat. Unlovely though the building was, the size of it impressed Mary. A score or more of children were playing outside, some engaged in a ball game, some scrambling up and down a mound of sand. Near the door, a trio of small girls worked industriously with an old broom to sweep dead leaves into the outlines of a playhouse.

None of these children was Tat, but a glimpse of faces at a window told Mary there were more youngsters inside. Her heartbeat quickened in spite of the warnings of her common sense. Among so many, wasn't it possible that one little boy in particular could be included?

"Netty!" The current wielder of the broom, a bandage covering one ear and the red blaze of a healing burn vivid across her cheek, halted in a swirl of crumbling leaves.

"Ruthie!" Netty chirped. She and Ruthie exchanged solemn smiles, gazing hard at each other.

Netty had not had a playmate nor anyone her own age to talk to except feverish, fire-crippled children for weeks, Mary realized. She responded without hesitation to the wistful loosening of Netty's fingers in hers. "You can go and play for a while if you like. Just don't go too far off. I'll call you when I'm done inside."

Netty's smile wavered uncertainly as if this were more than she had dared hope for. Then she slid her hands free of Mary's and Sigvard's and ran toward the leaf pile, looking rather like a windblown leaf herself in her yellow velvet.

A somber-eyed boy of about ten swung the door open to come out just as Mary and Sigvard were on the verge of opening it to go in. In reply to Sigvard's question, the boy directed them with a listless lift of the hand to a partitioned-off cubicle. There, Mr. Manning, a Peshtigo man who was acting as director of the orphanage, sat behind a litter of papers, ink bottles and pens at a scarred plank table.

"No, I'm sorry. There's no name like Cody here," Mr. Manning said after a brief scan of a list he unearthed from under a welter of other sheets. His regret sounded honest. "We have some sixty youngsters here, and nigh unto every one of them's been identified either by themselves or by friends or folks who knew them. If we had a Cody come in, you may be sure I'd get word to Ellery or your sister as fast as I could. That's the big part of my job here as I see it: tracking down relatives of these poor youngsters and trying to find families or homes for them."

Mary had known that her hope was anchored to reality by the frailest of threads. "But people are bringing more children here every day, aren't they? And if you have any who don't know their names—"

Mr. Manning wiped a negative hand down the front of the coarse, yellow coveralls he wore, probably a donation from a sawmill worker. "Not every day. Not like it was the first week or so. The last of our youngsters came, let's see—five days ago. There's been no new ones since. And four-year-olds like your nephew, mostly they know their names or enough about themselves to give us pretty good clues."

Mary nodded, feeling sympathy for Mr. Manning because he felt so sorry for her. "Tat would. He was a champion talker."

Was. It hurt to let go of that thread of hope. The ache would last for an immeasurable time. But there was endless aching, too, in fighting to hold fast a filiment of spider web.

"You think they are all here now or pretty close to all?" Sigvard asked. "All the stray children?"

"Most of them, I'd like to think. But people scattered so after the fire—to Oconto, Green Bay, the Peshtigo Harbor settlement, anywhere they could get to and find a place to stay. They took along any young ones that hadn't anyone to care for them. One fellow I know of is hunting his two-year-old in Chicago. He heard his boy was seen on a steamer headed for there, taken aboard by some well-meaning stranger who figured the lad was orphaned." Mr. Manning paused, tapping the finger of his left hand on the table. "You could see Lloyd Jones over in Menekaunee. He's got a little shaver at his place that nobody's claimed yet. I don't know too many of the details. Got my hands full keeping track of these—" he tapped the list in front of him "—but there's always an outside chance."

"Menekaunee, that's only a couple of miles from here," Sigvard said. "If you want to go, I can drive you there and back. I know a fellow will lend me a horse and rig."

"No." Mary drew back a step. She couldn't bear to reach for that spider's thread again and lose it. "Thank you, Sig, but surely Ellery knows about Mr. Jones. He's been to see Mr. Manning so often. And if he knows, then he's apparently learned the boy isn't Tat, for he's never mentioned it."

"Ellery Cody?" A pucker appeared at the corners of Mr. Manning's eyes. "It's possible he's heard of the Jones boy, but not from me. I see him once in a while out in front of the Dunlap House or sometimes on the dock when the steamers come in, but never to talk to much. I have to confess I didn't even know he'd lost a son." Mr. Manning's sigh carried apology and a weary regret. "There are so many . . ."

Mary closed her lips. Plainly, Ellery had not been here nearly every other day or any day at all.

A portion of her mind leaped to his defense: Ellery couldn't bear to come here day after day, knowing that the effort was pointless. He never had believed there was much cause to hunt for Tat among the living. But no defense was strong enough to smother her sense of betrayal. Ellery had lied to Clara and to her. He had simply pretended to act on Clara's wishes and then had done nothing.

There was a tremor in her voice that she could just barely control as she said, "In that case, I'd appreciate it if you could arrange to drive me out there, Sigvard. My sister will want someone to go, I know."

Five minutes later, she and Sigvard stood once more on the pine-slab doorstep, armed with Mr. Manning's careful directions and his sincere wish for good luck.

Only two little girls remained at work on the leaf house.

Netty and her friend Ruthie were nowhere to be seen. "They went around the other side of the church," the taller of the two girls volunteered.

"I'll fetch her," Mary told Sigvard hastily. "You were on your way to business of your own, weren't you? No need to lose any more time on our account. I can get us back safely to the Dunlap House myself, I'm sure."

She was even more sure that if she did not find a means of getting off alone soon where she could think, something drawn too taut within her was going to snap.

"*Ja*, well—" He probed her with a quizzical glance. "*Ja*, I'll go on then, if you are sure. I'll go find out about when we can have that horse."

Mary knew a fleeting gratitude as he turned away without further argument, leaving her to go on toward the church by herself. She heard the light sound of children's voices to the left and ahead. Deliberately she swerved to her right to take the long way around.

She was never quite positive afterward whether she actually did glimpse a flicker of yellow vanish through the church door when she reached the front. Or whether it was only her imagination inventing an excuse for her to step inside. In any event, the door was unlocked. It swung easily under her hand, whispering shut behind her.

The bright afternoon full of the whine of sawmills, the rattle of wheels, and the eyes of curious people was closed away. The tranquility of a place empty of everyone but herself breathed around her. For the first time since the fire, the first time in days past counting, she was really alone where there was no one to see her, no one to hear her, no one from whom she must screen her fears.

Her hands rose to the rough, dry texture of her cheeks, and she sank into a corner of the nearest pew. How could she live the rest of her life looking like this? Almost her every thought and act and word in the past had been shaped by the fact that she was pretty and that it pleased people to do her favors. Life would never be like that for her again.

Tears welled under the stub ends of her once-sweeping lashes and rolled over her fingers. She buried her face deeper in her palms and gave herself up to the storm of grief that had been building for such a long, long time. Her face . . . Tat . . . *The Lord hath afflicted me in the day of his fierce anger.* All because of her vanity and folly. All because of Ellery.

How she wished she had never set eyes on Ellery. She drew a quivering breath as the sobs began to lessen. Ellery, who fumbled at making decisions, who shrank from taking charge, who gladly followed anyone who would lead; Ellery, whose easy talk and easy manners sprang not from inner strength and confidence but from a habit of choosing the course of least resistance. How could she have been such a fool?

Mary wiped at her eyes with a corner of her shawl (handkerchiefs were a nicety that seemed not to have been included in any of the charity barrels of clothes), waking an angry glow in skin that was still tender. Despising Ellery and hating herself was not going to undo the damage that was done. Nothing was.

She sat a while longer, forcing herself to look hard into the frightening bleakness that like the seven lean cattle of the Bible had swallowed up the bright hopes of her future.

When she slipped out of the church at last, she found Netty sitting on the step. "I saw when you went in," Netty explained.

"Where's Ruthie?" Mary asked, for the other child was nowhere in evidence. "I thought you two were playing."

"I didn't want to any more. I told her I was tired." Netty stood up and tucked her hand into Mary's, ready to go.

Mary was too full of her own concerns to place much importance on a minor parting of the ways among children. Not until she and Netty were almost in sight of the square where the Dunlap House stood did she recognize that the little girl was more than usually subdued.

"Are you all right? Are your knees hurting?" Mary asked, slowing her pace. Her own newly healed burns on the soles of her feet were beginning to tell her that she had walked far enough.

"No." Netty's thumb went up into her mouth. She walked on, staring straight ahead over it.

"Ruthie is an orphan," she said suddenly. "She has to go and live with her uncle, and she don't want to. She don't like him. She don't like to be an orphan."

"I'm sorry about that. But things happen sometimes that can't be helped no matter how we like them," Mary said, and tried to ignore how sharply the truth still pinched.

Netty pulled her thumb from her mouth and studied it, not looking up. "Ruthie's Mama fell down and didn't get up. They were running when the fire came, and she fell down and didn't get up." The small hand tightened in Mary's. "I fell down, but my Mama didn't. My Mama's sick, but she's going to get well."

Mary gave the hand an understanding squeeze. "She's getting better every day. And your Papa isn't sick at all. You've got plenty of people to take care of you. You and Ida and your Mama and Papa and I, we're really pretty lucky."

Luckier than Ruthie, at any rate, and the dozens of other homeless orphans like Ruthie. Luckier than the nameless little boy in the home of Lloyd Jones. Luckier than Mr. Collins, who carried a tarnished gold ring set with a cracked and fire-blackened opal in his watch pocket, all that was left to him of his daughter. And who would spend the rest of his life looking after a wife who, except for her body, had died in the fire, too. Luckier than Arnold Robinson, dead with all his family in the ashes of their home.

It was a list almost without end, and one Mary had recited to herself more than once before, always finding it cold comfort. Yet, as she tumbled the comparisons through her mind this time, a new thought revolved to the surface: she would not trade the misfortunes she had to bear for those of anyone else she knew of.

"Yes," Netty said, eager to be persuaded, "we're lucky because Ida's cough is better, and Papa's going to find us a new little brother so Mama can get well, and then we'll get a house to live in and all be together. We'll be like before, won't we?"

The square little face framed by the beaver bonnet was so like Clara's in its sober earnestness, yet so unlike in its freshness and trust, that a rush of tenderness welled in Mary. She stooped and hugged the child right there on the street, oblivious to the glances of passersby.

"Don't you worry," Mary said, making it sound like the promise she was not believer enough to give.

Poor worn and tired Clara. Had *she* ever believed in promises that were as bright as butterflies and that carried no more weight?

Mary saw the answer in the blue-clad figure that left the veranda of the Dunlap House and started across the square to meet them as she and Netty reached the corner. It was odd that, rather than calling attention to his breadth and height, the ill-fitting coat managed to diminish the impressiveness of his size.

Mary's lips tightened with the reflection that he appeared to have got no farther toward finding them a place to live than the front steps of the hotel. Somehow, she had not expected that he would.

"Papa!" Netty greeted him.

Ellery caught her free hand, but his question was directed at Mary. "Where have you been?" He turned, tugging Netty onward. "I've been watching the street for you I don't know how long. Where have you been?"

Once such outspoken evidence that he wanted her nearby would have lifted Mary to the clouds. It was the final test of the change in her that now she felt only a jab of annoyance that their destination could have slipped his mind. "We told you where we would be: visiting the orphanage."

"I could have done that if it had to be done. Then you would have been here where you're needed."

He was hurrying them on toward the hotel at a pace that left Mary too short of breath to reveal that she was aware that he had done no such errand before. This wasn't the best moment for that, anyway. "Needed?" she panted. "For what?"

"It's Clara," Ellery said as they gained the boardwalk in front of the hotel. "It's—well—her time."

Dismay for herself and for Clara brought Mary to a standstill. "What can I do?"

She had been well shielded from the mysteries of birth even on the farm. What sketchy knowledge she did have was the product of watching ducklings and baby chicks break out of their shells and of ten forbidden and distressing minutes spent unobserved in the barn while her father and brothers were delivering a calf.

"I don't know," Ellery said. "The doctor's up there with her now and a couple of the women, I guess. But she'll want you near."

"Is she sick, Papa? Is Mama sick?"

Netty was gazing up at them through a peppering of freckles that were almost black against the sudden whiteness of her face. Mary clamped down on her own alarm in a flash of anger at Ellery. Did he have to be so thoughtless about how he broke the news? Didn't he understand how badly he could frighten a child who was already full of fears?

"It's not that your Mama's really sick," she told Netty, smiling as if she honestly had no doubts. "It's just that right now she needs some extra help to get well. And you heard your Papa say everybody is there with her, taking the best care they can. Everything will be fine. You wait and see."

She didn't blame Netty for looking unconvinced. It was such a long time since everything or anything had been fine.

"There's Ida," she said brightly as a little figure wrapped in yards of shawl toddled from behind a veranda post, dragging a string ahead of a capering, half-grown kitten. "You can tell Ida's not worried. Why don't you go play a while with her?"

"Yes, and keep an eye on her. Keep her out of mischief," Ellery said. "That will help Mama." He rubbed a hand across his forehead. "I was close to forgetting I had Ida out here with me."

He was little better than a child himself, Mary thought: only halfway dependable where there was any kind of distraction. Not that he didn't have cause to be distracted now.

The concession brought a shiver and made her conscious of an edge in the freshening wind. Soon it would be too cool for the children to stay outside. Then there would be the question of supper for them and settling them down for the night.

"Clara wants me upstairs near her, did you say?"

"Not that exactly. I don't know what's happening up there. It's best, though, not to get too far away. I couldn't tell much when I was up there. She never has an easy time of it . . . ."

And those other times Clara had been in reasonably good health, not weakened by smoke-damaged lungs and a system too recently undermined by exposure and shock. Mary swallowed to conquer dryness in her throat. "She'll be all right."

"Just stay near by." Ellery's hand pressed her elbow as if he would assist her onto the veranda, but he merely shifted from one foot to the other. "You can't tell. There's no knowing what to expect. Or when. That doctor knows what he's doing, of course. And Clara—Clara's been gaining ground pretty steady lately, don't you think?"

There he stood, his shoulders slightly hunched and the same appeal for reassurance in his eyes that had been in Netty's when she talked of being orphaned.

Mary could not go on hating anyone for whom she felt so sorry. She was needed here, she realized, but not by Clara at this moment; by him. Someone had to be here for Ellery to lean on, because he lacked the strength to stand alone.

And if something happened to Clara? If she didn't make it, he would probably go on leaning on Mary for as long as she would let him. He would be hers: her one-time daydream turned nightmare.

For if there was anyone she did not want anymore, it was Ellery. She would not have him if he were served to her on a silver platter.

Mary shaped for him the same falsely confident smile she had for Netty. She felt years older than she had at the start of this afternoon, older than Ellery would ever be.

"Everything will be fine," she repeated. Only this time it was a prayer.

Mary stirred drowsily in the big armchair, shifting her cramped legs and resettling her head on her bent arm. Her arm had gone numb from the pressure, although it was only minutes ago that she had curled herself up here to ease her weariness now that the long night of watching and waiting was over.

Almost over. There was still Ellery, whose restless anxiety had driven him out at last to pace the streets of the town in the early hours of the morning. That was why she had chosen this chair in the deserted lobby, so she could be sure to stop him when he came in and spare Clara the task of breaking the news to him that the son he had been counting on was a daughter.

Only the lobby was not deserted any more. Footsteps were tramping the length of it, ascending the stairs. Various voices were exchanging greetings and comments on the weather.

Mary sat up, rubbing her eyes. Somehow in the brief time between laying her head down and raising it again, the glow of the solitary lamp burning on the desk had been replaced by full daylight. Also, someone had draped a shawl over her. Her own shawl, she realized, as it slipped to the floor and she stooped to pick it up.

And there was Ellery, not just coming in but emerging from the dining room. Ida and Netty, looking newly washed and combed, were each clinging to a hand.

"Good morning, slug-a-bed," Ellery hailed her.

Mary scrambled to her feet in a flurry of embarrassment at having been caught asleep in a public place for all the world to see. "What time is it?"

"Past eight. You were dead to the world when I came in, and I didn't see any reason to wake you, tucked away in a corner like this. You'd had a hard night." He added as she began a hasty folding of the shawl, "Clara had me bring that down to you when I told her where you were."

"Clara— How is she? You've been in to see her?"

"Twice, this last time with the girls. She's doing fine, had a good breakfast and is sorting through a box of baby clothes that was in amongst the donation stuff." He grinned down at Netty and Ida. "The girls and I have had a good breakfast, too."

Ida nodded happily. "We gots baby."

"A baby sister," Netty explained, nodding too. "Mama got us a baby sister."

"I know," Mary smiled at her, but her glance was uncertain as she raised it to Ellery. "And you don't mind? That the baby's a girl, I mean?"

"Mind?" Ellery was strutting like the proudest of new fathers. "She's a beautiful little girl. Perfect. She is going to grow up to be the belle of the town just like her Auntie Mary."

Mary had never felt less like a belle of anywhere. Rather, she felt rumpled and grimy and in need of soap and water and a hairbrush.

Ellery, on the other hand, was as spruce and tidy as he was cheerful. Even the blue Army coat seemed to fit him better. No one would suspect he had passed a sleepless night. He was like the old Ellery before the fire, full of vigor and charm.

Mary's mood was brightened by the change in him. She had not dreamed that a new baby, and a girl at that, could affect him that much.

But she was not the old Mary, and his compliment stirred in her none of the old delight in herself or in him.

She gave him a tolerant smile that she might have used on one of her brothers, Grant or Wesley, and her attention shifted, unbidden, to his overcoat. "Are you going out again?"

He nodded. "As soon as Netty runs upstairs and fetches her wraps and Ida's. The girls think they'd like to come with me. I'm going over to see if the folks who've been housing the Collinses will let us have those rooms when Collins and his wife leave."

"I'll fetch them, Papa." Netty whirled away across the lobby and up the stairs.

Mary looked after her, then back at him, as bewildered as she was pleased. How long was it that he had been putting off this business of finding them a place to stay? And how long was it since he had last shown any real interest in the children?

Her surprise must have been obvious, for Ellery chuckled. "The steamer docked about an hour ago. I guess you were too sound asleep to hear the whistle. I suppose the Collinses will be on board her without too much delay. Oh, and I almost forgot." He slapped his coat pocket. "No, that's right, I left it with Clara. But she won't open it without you. It's addressed to you. A letter from your Pa."

Netty's scamper for the stairs was nothing compared to Mary's. A letter from Pa! She had scrawled a letter home on borrowed paper with a borrowed pencil a few days after her arrival in Marinette when she was at last able to use her bandaged hands.

There had been no guarantee, however, of when the letter would be delivered, much less of when she could expect a reply. Telegraph communication with the outside world had been destroyed by woods fires even before that terrible night in Peshtigo, so for all practical purposes it was only the steamers that plied between Marinette and Green Bay and Chicago that carried news out or brought it in. And the sailing schedules had been thrown into confusion for a time by the vessels and their captains doing their utmost to rush aid to the fire victims and to transport survivors to places of refuge as far off as Chicago. Yet it was said that on the night Peshtigo burned, Chicago, too, had been ravaged by a devastating fire.

Netty and Mary reached the top step at the same time. Together they entered the room where Clara lay resting against folded pillows. Netty darted ahead to crouch beside the blanket-lined dresser drawer that now filled the narrow space between Clara's bed and the next one.

"Here it is, Mary. See? See our baby?" Netty smiled as proudly as if the contents of the drawer were her own special treasure.

Mary was drawn irresistibly to her knees beside Netty. But she cautioned, "Hush, don't wake her. She's sleeping." Mary was not sure but what Clara, her eyes hidden behind the eyeshade, might not also be asleep.

Netty's voice became a hissing whisper that was hardly less carrying than her natural treble. "She's a girl," she said, repeating what to her apparently was the greatest of the marvel. "She's going to be my sister, and Tat can still be my brother. She doesn't have to be my brother."

"Tat will always be your brother," Clara said from the bed, "and nobody else will ever be Tat. This baby is herself and nobody else."

Mary considered telling Clara of the purpose of the drive she and Sigvard were planning to take later this day, but she decided against it. Why open another door to disappointment? That was what Ellery had said when she had told him of the plan. He had refused flatly to go along, nor had he offered any apologies for having avoided the orphanage all this time.

They had done a lot of talking last night, sitting together and drinking endless cups of coffee. Mary's sympathy for him had grown as her understanding deepened. He was not an unkind man, nor deceitful, nor calculating—that least of all, for calculation implied thinking ahead to probable consequences, something Ellery was rarely guilty of, be it in horse trading or promise giving. He was simply an ordinary man, a very ordinary man who could keep up as good a pace as any when he had a firm hold on both reins and a straight, clear road before him. But a man who stumbled to a helpless standstill when reins and road crumbled into ash.

"Your Papa will be leaving without you unless you hurry and get your bonnet on," Mary reminded Netty. In the wake of Netty's whirlwind scurry to collect the necessary items and depart, Mary explained to Clara where Ellery was going and why.

"I hope he does get the Collinses' rooms. I understand they are fairly comfortable, and it would be expecting too much, I suppose, to think the new house will be ready to move into before January."

"New house?" Mary asked.

Clara pushed herself higher on the pillows and raised the eyeshade a fraction. "Haven't you heard? The steamer brought the word this morning: the Peshtigo Company has decided to rebuild the town, commencing right away. Some of the men started back already, but Ellery won't be going until later, maybe tomorrow."

"No wonder Ellery's so happy," Mary said, and realized an instant too late how like a slur on Ellery it sounded. As if she believed that his wife's being safely delivered of a healthy daughter could not of itself account fully for such a remarkable restoration. Worse still, it was the truth.

"Ellery needs something definite to do," Clara said matter-of-factly. There was no trace of offense in her voice. "He's at his best when everything is laid out for him and he can go straight to work."

It was a woman-to-woman bit of frankness that sent a glow

through Mary that Ellery's empty flatteries never could. But it added to her discomfiture, too.

To hide her confusion, she knelt again beside the dresser drawer, and brushed a fingertip over the tiny fist that protruded from the mound of flannel. The baby opened round, blue eyes and a rounder pink mouth.

"I can see where I'll have my work cut out for me too," Clara said with a flicker of her old tartness. "Between you and Netty, she'll be spoiled rotten inside a week. Go ahead, pick her up if you want to. Maybe she'll hush."

Mindful of the other patients in the room, Mary did as Clara suggested, cuddling the now vigorously squirming bundle close to her in hopes of quieting the cries that sounded more experimental than complaining.

"Hush, hush," she crooned, rocking herself and the baby to and fro where she knelt, and the baby did hush. Unfocused eyes gazed up at her as if in wonder from a face crowned by a dusting of red-gold fluff, and a stretching arm waved a hand at her. It was adorned by the tiniest of fingers complete with perfect nails in miniature.

This is what it was all about, Mary thought in sudden awe. This is what Clara was waiting for. This is why I came here . . .

"What are you going to name her?" she asked.

"Grace," Clara said promptly. "I can't think of anything more fitting. She hasn't a flaw or a fault anywhere, and not a mark on her of any sort. Dr. May says that's an old wives' tale, thinking a baby will be marked by something that happens before it's born, but she's not his baby. I was so afraid she'd have some stamp of the fire on her somewhere."

Mary folded back the flannel wrappings for a better view of the sturdy little body, no longer angry red and wrinkled as she had seen it several hours ago, but faded to a soft healthy pink. Truly it did seem a miracle that in this hospital of the scarred and crippled and disfigured and dying, there could be one small human being, one tiny survivor of that fire, so completely whole and unscathed.

"Grace," she said.

Into her mind came the picture of a page of the Marinette and Peshtigo *Eagle*, printed in Marinette only a few days after the fire. In the space reserved for obituaries there had appeared only one name, with the printer's mark for mourning: Peshtigo.

"Grace Mary," Clara said.

Mary raised her head, doubting what she had heard.

Clara nodded. "For her aunt. She very likely wouldn't be here if it weren't for you. I couldn't have made it to the river that night, not if I'd had to carry Ida, too. And since then—" She tugged at the eyeshade, tipping it so that her eyes were hidden once more. "Well, what can I say? You've put me in mind of Ma at times—no complaining, never shirking . . ."

"Me? Like Ma?" Mary's breath caught on a small laugh that was not a laugh at all. To be likened to Ma, and by Clara? She rested her cheek against the downy top of the baby's head to quell an unreasonable impulse to cry. "I've got so much to make up for. If Ma ever dreamed how I—"

"No call to go into that," Clara cut in. "It's over and done with, and best forgotten."

Mary straightened. "It *is* over." Her arms tightened around the baby in her earnestness. "I swear it."

"I know." Clara waved a silencing hand at her. "My eyes may be too weak for reading, but there are some things I can see."

Mention of reading brought Mary scrambling to her feet. Clara must have had the same thought, for she was reaching under her pillow and drawing out an envelope in the same instant Mary exclaimed, "The letter! Ellery said we had a letter from Pa."

They looked at each other and began to laugh. Clara, Mary suspected, was as glad as she to find a ready excuse to put away an awkward subject.

Grace Mary Cody, weary of being squeezed, delivered a lusty kick toward her aunt's chin, and followed it by a lustier wail.

"I'll take her," Clara said. "You take the letter. It's addressed to you, but I confess my scruples might not have kept me from reading it if my eyes were stronger."

Mary settled herself on the foot of the bed to tear open the envelope. Three greenbacks slid from the folded sheet of paper she drew out.

"What's that? Money?" Clara asked in an interval between Grace Mary's yells. "Bless Pa! Bless him a thousand times over."

Mary nodded, but she gathered the notes into a safe pile in her lap without actually looking at them. Her eyes were already devouring the lines of Pa's thin, slanted handwriting in the letter, such frail yet precious links to a place where life remained normal and sure.

"They're coming here!" she exclaimed. "Pa and probably Ma, too, because he says she won't be talked out of it. They're going to take us home with them, every one of us, as soon as you're able to travel. That's what the money's for: to tide us over in the meantime and to pay for our fares."

She crushed the bills together in her left hand and sprang up, flourishing the letter like a banner in her right. "We're going home, Clara! Back to Sun Prairie and the farm!"

As much to her own surprise as Clara's, she swooped and planted a kiss on Clara's cheek. She was equally surprised by Clara's circling her in a tight hug with the arm unencumbered by the baby.

"Read it," Clara demanded. "Out loud. I want to hear every word."

Mary read it through to her not once but twice, delighting in each syllable. Even the baby, discovering how to nurse, subsided into small, contented sounds.

"To have Ma here," Clara sighed. "And Pa. To see them both again. It's too good to be true."

"And to go home again." Never had Mary supposed she would be jubilant at the prospect of sharing the comforts of the big farmhouse with Clara and her family, but she was. "Can you believe that? We're going home."

Clara was moving her head from side to side in a slow negative. "I can't go. Not now that Ellery has work to keep him here."

"Why not? You needn't stay just because Ellery does, you and the children. You could come back here in the spring when your house is done. We'd have the whole winter at home."

Clara adjusted the baby on her arm. "It would be glorious—" Her smile lost its momentary softness and took on a wry twist. "But you know me. If Ellery's going to be building me a house, I want to be right there supervising to be sure they get it done my way."

Or perhaps, that it got done at all, Mary reflected. Ellery might well lack the heart to hold any one goal steadily in view until it was accomplished. Clara was the backbone in his life. She was as necessary to him as she was to her children. The mystery of their marriage was as simple as that.

"But—" Mary folded Pa's letter carefully along the creases and unfolded it again. It was a waste of breath to argue further once Clara was set on something, yet this time *no* couldn't be the final answer. It couldn't.

"No buts. You just concentrate on going home yourself."

"You don't want me to stay here to help out?" Queer that the possibility should open an emptiness in Mary, when having to stay if Clara did was exactly what she was dreading.

"My conscience has enough to answer for on your account as it is. At least we'll be parting better friends than we were to start out, and maybe by parting better we can stay that way. That's worth a good deal to me, whether you think it or not. I'm not overly endowed with friends. Never was."

"We're—we're sisters," Mary said.

"We are that. I used to fancy I saw flashes of kinship in you even when you were little and I was living at home." Clara smiled thinly. "Not that there aren't aplenty that would hold that the resemblance is far to seek. I thought I'd come to terms with that a long time ago, but that was when you were just a youngster. If I weren't in a sentimental mood right now, I'd never admit this. But when you walked in through my front door the day you arrived, a grown young woman, you scared me."

"Scared you?" Mary's hands went automatically to her face. "I could now, yes. But when I first arrived?"

"Those scars will fade, given time, and your eyebrows are beginning to grow back already. You look a lot better today than you did a week ago. Whatever happens, I doubt you'll ever be reduced to quite the level of a plain woman." Once more the thin smile beneath the masking eyeshade. "I daresay you haven't driven behind the last wild horse that will be trotted through town to show you off."

Mary lowered her fingertips from a cautious tracing of her eyebrow. "You don't mean the mustang?"

" 'You can't expect a pretty girl to ride around behind an old sobersides like Dan. She wants a horse with style.' " Clara said, obviously quoting. She laughed unexpectedly. "Don't look so stricken. It wasn't your doing. He gave me a dozen other reasons as well, none of them the real one, which is that a horsetrader can't resist a good deal and Ellery can't resist a fractious horse. I know that now, and I knew it then, but I'm not noted for my sunny disposition at any time. And what with you making it clear you hated every minute you were here, and me feeling big as a hay wagon beside you and twice as clumsy . . . Well, let's say we both did our share of muddying the waters, and hope we're the wiser to pay for it."

Mary was at pains to spread the bills flat within the creases of the letter and to restore the whole to the envelope as if the promise they contained were only as substantial as the paper it was written on. Carefully, she said, "I'm wise enough to know that if you needed help in September, you'll need it considerably more through this winter."

"The best help will be knowing you're safe at home. There'll be dozens of hands to call on for any other help I want. Some of the women will be glad of something to do while they're waiting for their houses to be put up." Clara disentangled the front of her nightgown from Grace Mary's fist and eased the drowsing baby down beside her. Her face turned away from Mary, she added, "There are just the three children, anyway. I should be able to manage that."

Just the three. It was a refrain that kept running in Mary's head even as she stepped up into Sigvard's borrowed buggy to set out in search of Tat that afternoon. Her elation at the thought of going home was muted by it. Yet before the hotel was out of sight behind them, she was telling Sigvard of the letter in glowing detail.

Sigvard listened, nodding. "That is good news. Real good news for you. But do you think they both can come, your mother and your father? Who will look after the farm?"

"My brothers will. Wes has a place of his own and Grant lives in town, but Pa says they told him they would see that between them the chores get done." A gust of wind off the Menominee River which marked the northern boundary of the town impressed another fact on her. "It's almost November, so that makes it easier. There's not so much work to be done."

"*Ja*, that is a piece of luck" Sigvard agreed. "I was a farm boy until I was ten, until my father died. I know the good feeling after the harvest is in. But the best piece of luck," he went on quickly as if to forestall any sympathy or questions, "is to have such a fine, strong family like yours." He glanced down at her beside him. "I saw it must be such a family when you came that long way to help your sister."

Mary looked away. "I didn't come because I wanted to. I did everything I could to get out of it."

"I could see that, too," Sigvard said, unperturbed. "But you did come. That is what counts. And you did your share. It is good to have a family that stands together like that."

She bent her head. What evidence would it take to persuade him she seldom acted from the lofty motives he liked to credit to her? Suppose one day she should fall in his esteem as Ellery had in hers. Could that matter to her very much, since shortly she would be far removed from here and him? The answer was as definite as the dappled horse in front of her: it could, and would.

As the road led them out of Marinette, an elusive taint in the wind brought her to sharp attention. At first it was only a whiff here and there, but it thickened quickly into an almost solid presence in the air, the acrid and too-familiar smell of ashes and charred wood.

"Which way are we going?" she asked. "This isn't the road back to Peshtigo, is it?"

Even as she spoke, the trees on either side of the road were thinning. Scorch marks blackened trunks and heavy limbs.

"No, Peshtigo is south. We are going east. But the fire came this way, too. It split in two at the sandhills between Marinette and Peshtigo. Half went on up through the west edge of Marinette, and the other half, the worst half, went through Menekaunee."

The dappled horse was carrying them into a graveyard of

trees. Fallen trunks, their limbs burned away, littered the blackened ground. Some were mere shells of ash, already sunken and partly scattered by the winds and rain. An occasional black skeleton still stood upright, gaunt and desolate.

Mary linked her fingers tightly in her lap, fighting an upsurge of panic. This was nightmare come to life: the plodding horse, the hopeless, ruined landscape without beginning or end. She was gripped by a fear that if she turned her head, she would see that nameless, faceless driver of her dream beside her, driving her relentlessly on into a haze of uncharted dread.

"Menekaunee. That's the village we're going to, isn't it?" She had to swallow to get the words out. "It wasn't burned much?"

"It was burned pretty bad, so I heard. Thirty-some houses, fine new sawmill, a shipyard, a couple of hotels—all burned. But none of the people. They got on a ship, a lot of them, and stood out in the middle of the river until it was over. Not all the buildings were lost, either, I guess, or we would be going somewhere else to look up Mr. Lloyd Jones."

The voice was Sigvard's, warm and unruffled as usual, and as always tinged with a hint of what she was beginning to recognize as amusement. The face was his too, long and bony and strong. It was not a face that would dissolve into mist and leave her frightened and alone.

Her panic ebbed. She made herself smile in reply to his smile. It was not enough, though, to restore the brightness of her earlier mood. A grayness had seeped into her like a reflection of the afternoon's pewter sky.

They were coming up on the remains of a house and barn now, although it was difficult to tell which had been which. Nothing was left but the blackened fieldstones of the foundations. Peshtigo would look like this when Clara returned. It would be a long while before new houses and new activity could erase the last traces of that night's terror. How could Clara bear it?

"They say some of the ministers are preaching that Peshtigo was burned because it was a wicked town. It's God's judgment on us," she said. "Have you heard that?"

"I am not much of a churchgoer. When I went to services, it was mostly to please my aunt. But if that is the kind of nonsense they are preaching, all the more reason to stay away."

That was the answer Pa might have given, Mary realized. He was not much of a churchgoer, either. But the question had been eating at her too long to let it go at that. "How can you be sure it's nonsense? Don't you believe people are punished for their sins?"

"I think that to burn hundreds of innocent men and women and little children to death is a strange way to punish other people for their sins. That is not my idea of justice. It is not even common sense." There was a quality of confidence in his way of speaking today that was new. It was as if he had grown more sure of himself, of what he thought and what he believed, and more sure of her, too, no longer wary of how she might respond.

"But don't you think that people who seem innocent and decent to their neighbors could be secretly guilty of doing something terribly wrong?" Mary persisted. "Maybe there were those who were deserving of judgment, and only they knew it."

Sigvard slanted a quizzical glance at her. "What I think is that if there is any good in them, they will do their own punishing. It wouldn't need the waste of a whole forest and town and a thousand lives to settle the score." His tone was partly teasing, partly serious. "When I was in school, our teacher read us a story once about a man who went looking for the one sin God could not forgive. In the end, the answer was his own pride in thinking he, who was just a man, had more power to do evil than God did to do good."

Hawthorne, Mary thought. She had read that story, too. At the time, she had dismissed it as just a dreary tale, but perhaps there was more in it to ponder than she had recognized then. She let the subject drop until she could sort her thoughts more clearly.

The fire must have raged through Menekaunee as fiercely as it had through Peshtigo. There were rectangles of blackened debris where houses had stood. Gaping cellar holes and mounds of ash marked the sites of other buildings. But the village was not a deserted place as she had been imagining Peshtigo to be. Soot-smudged crews of men were at work here and there raking through the ashes, clearing away the rubble, and in one place hammering together the framework of a new house above the stone foundation of the old. Incredibly, some few houses on the farther outskirts were still standing, smoke-stained but otherwise undamaged. It was toward one of these that a workman directed Sigvard when he stopped beside the house-building crew to ask the way to Lloyd Jones's.

Mary closed her eyes an instant and willed her heartbeat to an unhurried rhythm as the buggy drew up in front of the house. All through the drive, she had kept her mind resolutely away from Tat. She did not expect to find him here any more than Ellery did. Her hand was as cold as stone, but far less steady, in the warm grasp Sigvard offered to help her to the ground. How many times would she go through this again before she left for home? And how many times after that would Clara?

A sandy-haired boy of about eight answered Sigvard's knock. He bobbed a silent nod in acknowledgment that this was Lloyd Jones's house and stared round-mouthed from Mary's face to Sigvard's tall hat while Sigvard attempted to explain their errand.

"Who is it, Owen?" a woman called from somewhere in the house.

The boy whirled and dashed off in the direction that was probably the kitchen, leaving Mary and Sigvard on the stoop. "It's folks come to get Georgie, Ma."

The tight band across Mary's chest relaxed. Georgie. She no longer had to struggle against the danger of beginning to hope. There remained only to make excuses to the Joneses for disturbing them, and she and Sigvard could start back to Marinette.

Owen's mother, a roly-poly woman not much taller than he and as sandy of complexion, bustled along the hall toward them, trailing an aura of strong laundry soap and steam.

"Come in, come in!" She reached to pull the door wider for them with one hand and tuck a stray lock of hair off her flushed face with the other. "I'm Mrs. Jones. Come in, come in out of the cold. You're going to find everything here at sixes and sevens, I'm afraid, but it seems like I'm up to my ears these days just trying to keep this family in clean clothes when anything they touch is inches thick in soot. You're here about the little boy?"

"Yes," Mary said. "That is, I'm not sure. We're looking for my little nephew."

She went on to introduce herself and Sigvard and to do what she could to explain further as Mrs. Jones ushered them into a small parlor that was in apple-pie order for all her apologies.

"Four years old, you say? That's about right." Mrs. Jones nodded, waving them to a horsehair sofa while she nearly vanished into the depths of a wing chair. "I'd have guessed closer to three, but at that age, it's hard to tell. He has the blue eyes and blond hair, what's left of it. It was singed so bad that I sheared most of it off when Mr. Jones brought him home." She leaned around one of the chair wings to address a freckled girl peering in at them from the hall. "Go get Georgie, Margaret. It's time he was up from his nap, anyway."

"No, wait," Mary said. "If his name is Georgie—"

"We don't know what his name is. We haven't a clue. Georgie is what we've been calling him for want of anything better, and he's got so he answers to it well enough. If he didn't, I'd swear the poor little mite was a deef-and-dumb, for he hasn't uttered a sound since he's been here. Not even the day he pinched his finger in the drawer. Just stood there, big tears rolling down his cheeks and not a whimper." Mrs. Jones spread her fingers, shaking them and rocking slightly as if she could feel the pain herself.

"You said your husband brought him here?" Sigvard asked. "Where did he find him?"

"Mr. Jones was down at Peshtigo Harbor the night of the fire. Thank God it didn't burn that far east, and thank God this house was a hairsbreadth outside its path, too. The paint on the west side is blistered from the heat. Well, anyway—" Mrs. Jones moved herself forward to the edge of the chair—"Mr. Jones went up from the harbor to the town as soon as he could the next day, and there in the midst of nothing, big as life, was this little bit of a boy. Nobody with him, not a mark on him except, like I said, his hair was singed and the soles of his little shoes were nearly scorched through from wandering around in those hot ashes. All Mr. Jones could get out of him was a couple of croaks that didn't amount to anything—you know how hoarse that smoke made everyone—and he couldn't find a soul that seemed to know who the boy was or could tell him a jot about him. So there wasn't much else to do but bring him home to look after until somebody from his family came hunting him. If he had any family left."

Mary turned her head, alert to the clatter of footsteps on uncarpeted stairs. She had a cowardly desire to leave without setting eyes on Georgie. He would not be Tat; he must not be. To think of Tat's having undergone such an ordeal as this child did, to think of any child's having to suffer it, was too awful to dwell on.

"Has anyone else come by to ask about him?" she questioned, for the sake of shifting the subject.

"A few. A man looking for his son and an older couple looking for their grandchild. The hard part is that they go away so disappointed."

Mary wondered if Sigvard were feeling the same dismay as she, for he asked, "What will you do if no one ever claims him?"

"Keep him, of course." Mrs. Jones's chuckle intimated that the answer was so obvious as to be ridiculous. "We have six of our own. One more would be hardly noticed. In fact, he's the least trouble of the lot: no noise, no mischief, no fussing, never gets himself dirty." She aimed a playful nudge at Owen, who was leaning against her chair arm, drinking in every word.

It's not Tat then, it can't be, Mary told herself, as a flutter of giggles and whispers collected near the door. Three freckled girls appeared, almost identical except for a variation in heights. Ahead of them they were herding a smaller child who neither resisted their proddings nor advanced any farther by himself when they retreated from him in the center of the room.

Mary caught her breath. "Tat?" she said uncertainly.

He lifted unwinking blue eyes to her at the sound of her voice, and her uncertainty grew. It wasn't merely that instead of unruly gold curls, his head was covered by scarcely better than a blond fuzz. Neither was it that the face that should have been rounded and rosy was pallid and thin. It was the expression on his face—or rather, the lack of expression—that labeled him a stranger. There wasn't the faintest twitch of a muscle to hint at recognition. The eyes gazing mildly at her were totally empty of interest or concern or, for that matter, comprehension. Empty of anything.

She bent to hold her hand out to him. "Tat. Don't you remember me? It's Mary. And Sigvard. Don't you remember Sigvard?"

"Go on, Georgie, shake hands," prompted the youngest girl in a whisper. She darted forward to jog his elbow so that his hand plopped onto Mary's palm. He let it lie there, limply curved, as if one resting place were as acceptable as any other for it.

Mary peered into the unresponsive face that might as well have been an ivory carving. He was like Tat, very like him, yet he was also so unlike him that she could be persuaded the resemblance was only superficial. Which mistake would be the more monstrous: to lay claim to the wrong child or to turn her back on the right one? She threw a glance of appeal at Sigvard.

Sigvard stretched a long arm to circle the boy's shoulders and draw him closer. "What about horses, Tat? You still would like to drive your papa's horses, *ja*?"

The child's eyes moved to him as they had to Mary and drifted on indifferently to the rounded back of the sofa, the framed array of dried flowers above it, the painted lamp on a table at the sofa's end.

"What's that you call him?" Owen asked. "Tat?"

"Tat," Mary said. "The name is Stanton, but it always came out Tat when he tried to say it, so Tat is what everyone calls him."

"Tat!" Margaret, the biggest of the girls, sprang to sudden

animation. "Ma, that's what Dad said it sounded like when he asked him his name. He said Georgie made a sound like Tat every time he asked him, only Dad didn't think Tat could be a name. He thought he was maybe just trying to cough."

"That's right, Dad did tell us that. None of us took it for anything but gibberish, and of course, he hasn't made a sound since that. But that's his name then: Tat. That must be it." Mrs. Jones was bobbing her head in delight. "What a shame Mr. Jones has to be across the river hauling lumber today. He'll be so tickled when he hears that Georgie and his folks have found each other."

But had they? Might not it have been a cough indeed, the scrape of a smoke-raw throat, that Mr. Jones had interpreted as Tat? Mary still was not absolutely convinced, but now neither could she contemplate leaving the child behind.

"If I know my sister," Mary said, "she'll be here to thank you herself as soon as she is up and around. She expects to be well enough to leave the hospital in another week or so."

Mrs. Jones was patting the hem of her apron to her eyes, all the while smiling a smile that bunched her cheeks into apple bulges above it. "A miracle, that's what it is. A real, honest-to-goodness miracle and no two ways about it. Owen, stop that cavorting in here. You, too, Margaret. Winnifred, Susan—"

Owen continued efforts to chin himself on the high back of his mother's chair and his sisters continued to laugh and poke at him as if they had not heard. In the midst of the hubbub, the little boy who might be Tat stood leaning against Sigvard's knee as if he did not hear or see, either. His hand still lay in Mary's. Sigvard reached over to cover it with his own strong fingers, giving Mary's a brief pressure that spoke more than any words of understanding.

"But what am I thinking of, just sitting here doing nothing?" Mrs. Jones rolled herself to her feet. "His mother will be wanting the clothes he was wearing, and by luck, they're all washed and pressed. I darned up the burn holes, and there's plenty of wear left in them, except the shoes, but Davy's old ones are a pretty good fit, so that's all right. Davy and Sam, those are my youngest, twins, are down making life lively for their grandparents in Oconto this week. I have a number of things they've outgrown I'll send along."

She did better than that. Besides the generous assortment of boys' garments she bundled up, she outfitted the child in a wool cap against the cold and a somewhat oversized sheepskin jacket that looked almost new. She provided a handkerchief to wipe away the tears that persisted in sliding down Mary's face.

Snow was falling in lazy, big flakes when Mary and Sigvard, the little boy between them, tucked themselves under the bearskin robe that was part of the buggy's equipment, and started on the return road to Marinette. Mary pointed the snowflakes out to the child as they landed on his lap or his sleeve, and she talked to him of Ida and Netty and his Mama and Papa and of going home, repeating herself over and over without result. Except that he blinked when an occasional snowflake struck his eyelashes, and that now and then he shifted his legs under the bearskin or righted himself when a bump in the road jounced him off balance, he appeared as oblivious to his surroundings as was the box of clothes at his feet.

Mary sighed and gave up. This was far from an unmixed blessing they were about to bestow on Ellery and Clara, this restoration of their missing child. How was Clara ever going to manage alone with this added burden?

"Maybe it will be different when he sees his mother and sisters and his father, do you think?" she asked Sigvard. "I shouldn't expect him to recognize me, really. I've changed so. But they're not that much altered."

Sigvard looked at her as if for the first time he was assessing the extent of the change that had been wrought. She wished intensely that she had not mentioned it. All he said, however, was: "It will take time, maybe. And patience. And love."

He made no gallant denial that she was changed, she noted. She studied the rim of snow that was thickening along the edge of the dashboard and sought for a more comfortable topic. "You haven't said anything about your farm today. Have you done any more thinking about it?"

"The farm is mine. Tomorrow the papers will be drawn up. I am to pay whatever I feel is fair and whenever I feel I can, but to work, to live on, the farm is mine right now."

"Sigvard! I'm so glad for you." She slipped her arm around the little boy and gave him a small hug of pleasure. "You won't be sorry, I'm sure."

"No, I won't be sorry. All my life what I've wanted is to have a home and a family of my own. This is the beginning. Also yesterday I signed on to a logging crew to do blacksmithing, which means maybe there will be money for seed in the spring." Pride shone in his deep-set eyes, but a hint of the old shyness tempered his smile. "It was your advice that persuaded me, you know. Are you ready for such a responsibility?"

Mary felt herself blushing without knowing why. Shyness must be catching. She was startled by a thrust of envy for the girl who would some day win the right to share his future on that farm and help make his dream come true. Well might that girl count herself lucky.

"I'll always be interested in how things are going for you," she said to the crown of the boy's cap.

"Maybe, then," Sigvard said as if he were taking care in the selection of each individual word, "you would not mind if once or twice I wrote you a letter? Would you answer from Sun Prairie?"

"Yes, I'll answer." Mary paused. "But not from Sun Prairie. I'll be staying here as long as Clara needs me."

"You won't go home with your parents? You are sure?"

"I'm sure." She couldn't say when the decision had crystallized, but she did not have to think about it to know that it was firm, unalterable. Ma and Pa would go back home without her. None of Clara's token protests could prevail.

She laughed to hide the wrench that the realization cost her. "I can't go home looking like this. My friends would be afraid to come near me."

Sigvard regarded her thoughtfully as he had before, and shook his head. "Can they be such fools?" He touched a finger to her cheek and very gently drew it across the roughened skin. "I think that you have never been more beautiful."

Finger and cheek both were snow-chilled, but within her a warmth like summer glowed and spread. For some reason she was remembering the curves and living weight of the baby her arms had held this morning, and the quiet undernote of pride in Clara's voice when she had said she had to be where Ellery was. It was a joy to be beautiful and admired, but there were gifts that struck deeper and held more substance: Being needed by someone. Being wanted.

Mary hugged the little boy to her again, her heart aching nonetheless. At the same time she was happier than she could remember ever being before, happy to be Mary James.

The snow was falling faster. Already the charred landscape ahead and behind and to either side of them was growing white. In another hour or two the scars of the fire would be all but obliterated by the snow.

Sigvard gave the reins a shake to free them of clinging snow. The horse quickened its jogging pace to a trot.

The boy stirred against Mary's arm. His chin came up. The sound he made was rusty, tentative, indistinct. It might have been a cough, but then, again, it might have been—one day perhaps it would become—"Giddap."

About the Author

BEVERLY BUTLER, a native of Milwaukee, Wisconsin, began writing stories at fourteen, partly for typing practice so that she could rejoin her high school class after losing her sight. Her *Light a Single Candle*, which won the Clara Ingram Judson Award, and *Gift of Gold* are both based on her own experiences.

Her first novel, *Song of the Voyageur*, won Dodd, Mead's *Seventeenth Summer* Literary Competition, and her most recent story was *A Girl Named Wendy*. Beverly Butler was graduated from Mount Mary College and holds an M.A. degree from Marquette University. She has received the Johnson Foundation Prize of the Council of Wisconsin Writers, and divides her time between writing and teaching creative writing courses.

She is married to Theodore V. Olsen, also a writer. They live in Rhinelander, Wisconsin.